## Praise for *Defensible Spaces*

"I wait for Alison Turner's fiction th...  t
after a long period of darkne...
A beautiful, soul-touching ti...
explores—with grace and preci...
former mining community in C ... ...avor,
one that carries our world, and c... ...you'll be reaching for again
and again."

—PAUL YOON, author of *Run Me To Earth*

"Alison Turner's stories are embers. They spark and glow. They smolder for years, sparing some lives while devastating others when they burst back into flame."

—ERICA OLSEN, author of *Recapture and Other Stories*

"In this masterfully woven collection, Alison Turner exposes the human kindling in a community racing to stay one step ahead of fire. The residents of Clayton, Colorado, are diverse, compelling, broken, and haunted, and Turner brings to their lives an incisive awareness of an environment's ephemerality. Combining a tender evocation of place and a compassion for human frailty, *Defensible Spaces* points to the future of fiction."

—KATY SIMPSON SMITH, author of *The Everlasting*

"Small-town life in Colorado has not been this riveting or beautifully wrought since Kent Haruf's *Plainsong* trilogy. In *Defensible Spaces*, we meet residents from the mountain town of Clayton: post office workers and bus drivers, liquor store clerks and pregnant mothers, firewood dealers and photographers, all of them engrossed in lifelong relationships with each other as Clayton itself seems ready to catch fire at any moment. With empathy and clear-eyed tenderness, Turner invites us into their tenuous lives with all the delicacy of her carefully tended prose."

—BLAKE SANZ, author of *The Boundaries of Their Dwelling*

defensible spaces

# defensible spaces

STORIES BY
ALISON TURNER

TORREY HOUSE PRESS

Salt Lake City • Torrey

First Torrey House Press Edition, February 2023
Copyright © 2023 by Alison Turner

Published by Torrey House Press
Salt Lake City, Utah
www.torreyhouse.org

International Standard Book Number: 978-1-948814-67-6
E-book ISBN: 978-1-948814-68-3
Library of Congress Control Number: 2021952962

Cover photo by Katie Crow
Cover design by Kathleen Metcalf
Interior design by Rachel Buck-Cockayne
Distributed to the trade by Consortium Book Sales and Distribution

Torrey House Press offices in Salt Lake City sit on the homelands of Ute, Goshute, Shoshone, and Paiute nations. Offices in Torrey are on the homelands of Southern Paiute, Ute, and Navajo nations.

The Merrill County Fire Department is always looking for volunteers to join our team! As a volunteer, you may be asked to assist in emergency extinguishing efforts as well as ongoing mitigation programs that support healthy forests and a safe Wildlife Urban Interface environment for all Merrill County residents. Among other initiatives, mitigation efforts include the Defensible Spaces Campaign, est. 2002, that supports homeowners with removing combustible debris down to the requisite fuel density for the full radius of the Home Ignition Zone, a minimum of 120 feet from all standing structures.

As of 2010, we are excited to offer a new volunteer opportunity to assist with community education and outreach. In an ongoing effort to increase resident compliance with fire bans, prescribed burns, and evacuation procedures, it is our hope that growing a network of informed and engaged volunteers will spark a fanning effect of fire prevention awareness and a decrease in arson and negligence across Merrill County, Colorado.

*Merrill County Fire Department Volunteer Handbook,*
*p. 2, updated 2014*

# — Contents —

Lifted Fire Ban ——————————————————— 1

Combustible Debris ——————————————— 13

Mitigation ————————————————————— 27

Fuel Density ——————————————————— 41

Defensible Spaces —————————————— 55

Home Ignition Zone ————————————— 69

Fanning Effect ————————————————— 89

Wildlife Urban Interface ————————— 103

Evacuation ————————————————————— 117

Prescribed Burn ————————————————— 131


Acknowledgments —————————————— 145

About the Author —————————————— 147

About the Cover Photo ———————————— 149

# — Lifted Fire Ban —

## 1991

*We burned our history.*

Bonnie Hadford sits in a folding chair in the newly-cleared field of dirt that will soon hold the new home of someone rich from somewhere else, thinking about what her husband said. It was dramatic, as always, and without expansion. And what did he mean by *we*?

She hasn't seen him, Roy, since this morning, when she returned with the news that the headframe to the old Red Bird Mine and the neighboring museum have burned down. Red Bird started as a silver mine in the 1890s. Decades ago, they filled in the shaft and made the headframe the center of Red Bird Park; three years ago they added a mining museum next to the original structure. The Red Bird Mine is the reason Clayton, Colorado, exists.

Two tiny and bright fires begin to sizzle. Bonnie's daughter and her daughter's best friend twirl while holding sparklers, encasing themselves in thin beams of light.

"Girls?" Bonnie says.

They do not hear her through their spinning.

"*Elizabeth*," Bonnie says.

Elizabeth stops twirling and looks at her mother, crumbs of light falling from her stick onto the dirt.

"Karly," Bonnie says.

Elizabeth's friend stops twirling but continues humming.

"How did you light those?" Bonnie says.

The girls stare at her, swaying. They met in kindergarten last year and strangers assume they are sisters. They both have long hair that neither of them will let anyone brush, freckles, and natural abilities to climb trees and rocks. But they are different at their cores: it is always Karly, then Elizabeth.

"The lighter," Karly says. She returns to spinning, drawing electric loops. The candle lighter sits on top of the open box of sparklers near one of the totes that they, mostly Bonnie, hauled down the road. Bonnie has never taught Elizabeth how to use a lighter. More and more, Elizabeth knows things that Bonnie has nothing to do with.

"Next time ask me first," Bonnie says.

"Okay," Karly says.

"Okay," Elizabeth says.

Bonnie puts the lighter under her thigh and settles back into her chair and the rhythm of Gus Lucero chopping wood. A widower with two sons and a firewood business, Gus is the Hadfords' only neighbor, for now. He was out late last night with the volunteer fire department trying to *save our history*, as Roy might say. Last night, Bonnie couldn't get to sleep until she heard the thwap of Gus's truck door. Sometimes, when their schedules align, his ax steadies her day, the metronome for her time at the sink, at the clothesline, while putting away groceries, when staring at the grove of aspen outside the kitchen window.

This is the wettest year in half a decade, and the first time in Elizabeth's lifetime that they've lifted the fire ban, which means the town can shoot fireworks over the reservoir for the Fourth. Like anyone else living in Clayton, Bonnie knows that a fire could catch any year, no matter what the accumulated rainfall.

As if to prove it, one did. This morning, while taking photos of what used to be the Red Bird, police tape kept her from getting close enough to get the shot she wanted. Half the remaining structure was a deep, velvety black in swooping curls. People are saying arson.

Roy comes from a heritage of mining the Red Bird, and when the museum opened three years ago, Bonnie convinced him to donate his boxes of photographs, letters, and a tool or two to the collection. Now he assumes the worst, like he always does, that everything he donated is gone. But, Bonnie tried to tell him, the strangest things survive fires. He had no response to that. He had already started wandering off with his decades-old water canteen, which maybe could have made it into the museum. When he takes the canteen, it means that no one should expect him back until evening. He hates the Fourth, anyway. Fireworks make him wince.

The girls crouch by the tote bags, rummaging in the box of sparklers. Karly looks for the lighter while Elizabeth stares at the colors on the sparkler box. Finally, Karly says, "Can you light these?" and Bonnie does. Twirling with their new sparklers, their oversized T-shirts, navy blue on Elizabeth and lime green on Karly, billow.

Bonnie never would have gotten sparklers. But when she picked up Karly from her grandma's, Karly got in the car holding the long thin box and talking impossibly fast about how her grandma promised she could light them. Bonnie would have asked the other parent before making that kind of promise, but that was just one of the differences between herself and Cheryl Krane. Cheryl works at the post office with Roy, though the only thing he's ever said about her is that she has a drinking problem but doesn't let it stop her. She and Karly live in the trailer park and every time Bonnie picks up or drops off Karly, the lot is crowded with people smoking on steps beneath strapped-open doors or sitting in chairs in the middle of the road. Sometimes

Cheryl is nowhere in sight and one of the neighbors calls Karly over and that is that. But if Cheryl is there, she traps the girl in a loud, endless hug.

It was after coming home one day from Karly's that Elizabeth first said *I love you.* Bonnie loves Elizabeth in a way that leaves her speechless, but she and Roy never said it out loud until Elizabeth did. The first day Elizabeth said it, as easy as she might say *I brushed my teeth,* Bonnie said it right back. Now, both she and Roy say it to Elizabeth but never to each other.

She pulls a tote full of sandwiches onto her lap, plucks at one of the baggies, then puts the whole thing back on the ground. Bonnie invited Gus, his boys, and his visiting brother and nephews to join her and the girls in watching the fireworks: this is the last year the Hadfords and the Luceros will have their view of the reservoir, since the new house will be large enough to block it. *I'll make sandwiches,* she'd said. They hadn't said yes for sure, but she stacked the chicken, the tomato, the knife with the mayo, in rhythm to Gus chopping wood, making sandwiches until the bread ran out.

She wants to turn around and watch through the trees Gus splitting wood, each hit like a heartbeat, but she faces the reservoir and tries to be satisfied with listening. The reservoir is still as a plate. The sun is starting to set but they still have half an hour before the mountains take all the light. Next month, loaders and trucks and construction crews will dig and drill and honk and pull up the ground she sits on. The Hadfords are 60 Tungsten Drive, the Luceros 110, and the new place, where Bonnie sits right now, will be 600. Roy says the numbers are designated by the fire service, that every 100 means a tenth of a mile from the main road. She never knows how Roy, who never talks to anyone, knows these things.

The chopping stops. Bonnie refuses to turn to see if they are coming (a game she played as a kid and now plays with Elizabeth: hold your breath, your hand out the window in the winter, your gaze away from something you want to see, as long as you can). There is a flair of noise behind her of pretend explosions and whacks, a displacement of air that only a group of boys can make. The sun drops with incomprehensible smallness and the blue of the water deepens.

"Don't throw rocks."

Gus Lucero's voice.

"What'd I say?" Gus again.

"Yes, sir." That was Ross, Gus's twelve-year-old son.

She breathes out and turns. Gus and his brother, Luke, each carry a folding chair in one hand and a six-pack in the other. A dog sniffs at their feet as they walk, and the boys swarm behind, some of them still throwing rocks high into trees, half of them carrying plastic milk gallons full of water and heavy-looking bags. Gus, tall and thin, a black beard and big boots, takes long, calm strides; his brother is shorter and has bulkier muscles. They are both tidy but rugged, like you can't scrub the work off of them.

"Hello, Bonnie." Luke puts out his hand and smiles. "You get some shots of the Red Bird today?"

"Hi, Luke." His hand is wide and has the same amount of rough as Gus's. "I tried. It's a beautiful mess."

The brothers screech open their chairs splotched with rust.

"I bet they never catch the guy," Gus says.

"Probably kids," Luke says.

"Think they'll keep what's left standing?" Bonnie says.

"I bet it collapses before they can decide," Gus says. "When we left last night I didn't think it'd make it to morning."

Bonnie craves her camera from the way the falling shadows clothe parts of Gus but leave his arms bare. She used to take pictures for herself, moments she wanted to keep for no reason but to see them again, but more and more the photos are for someone else: parents of kids on the volleyball team who want to see their athletes in the *Clayton Clamour*; Elizabeth when she is older, even though she already hates having her picture taken; the town of Clayton, who will want documented the end of the Red Bird Mine.

"Ready for sandwiches?" she says, suddenly embarrassed by how many she made. She passes them each a plastic baggie before they can answer.

A silence drops slowly but it won't hit the ground—the memory of Gus's wife always catches it. When Annie and Gus Lucero and a little boy named Ross built the place next door, Bonnie wasn't working much, and whenever she felt lost and needing purpose, she often walked over to help Annie with cooking, cleaning, diapers. They talked or they didn't talk and the days went by fast, hours turned to connective tissue between moments that were short in time but endless in other dimensions: the time they needed to squeeze into the small pantry and bring down the crockpot from the top shelf and their bodies turned to each other, almost pressing; the times sitting next to each other on the soft scarlet sofa that Bonnie can still feel in her inner elbow, her lower back, her upper neck.

Annie died giving birth to her second son, Tyler, two years before Elizabeth was born. Bonnie still gets waves of dizziness with Annie gone, moments that sway her after eight years. She sees the swaying in Gus, too, and sometimes it steadies when they are together, as if their disorientations cancel each other out.

"Only on the dirt, like I said," Bonnie calls to the girls. They had moved to the far edge of the build site, still swirling with sparklers. Bonnie reaches for the lighter and it is gone—it sits on top of the sparkler box. Karly must have snuck in when Bonnie was distracted by the Luceros.

Karly's baggy T-shirt is now twisted up to her belly button, a bright green bikini.

"I was wondering if they'd cancel the show because of the Red Bird fire," Bonnie says.

"No way," Gus says. "They've already spent too much money."

"Roy coming later?" Luke says.

"He's not feeling well," Bonnie says.

"He still at the post office?" Luke says. The last time Luke visited, his wife also came, and Roy helped her mail medication back to someone in Nebraska, priority. Bonnie doesn't know where Luke's wife is now, but something tells her she isn't waiting back home. The boys are too rowdy and Luke too tired.

"Sure is," Bonnie says. She does not want to talk about Roy, or how he used up his vacation days to do nothing but wander around so that now they can't take Elizabeth to the Grand Canyon, or how last week he promised to build a tree swing with Elizabeth and got everything ready, rope, plank, hammer, nails, drill, all under the tree they'd chosen, then disappeared for the rest of the afternoon.

She used to not care how he used his vacation days. For most of their life together, they didn't know each other's schedules or wait for each other for dinner if they didn't feel like it. But it is different now that there is Elizabeth. Bonnie has to tell him when she'll be back and, worse, ask when he will be.

"How are the boys?" she says. From this distance, Bonnie can barely tell Ross and Tyler from Luke's three sons. All of them have dark, messy hair, and skinny, fast-moving limbs.

Both men make a dismissive sound in their throats and Bonnie laughs. She moves her long ponytail over her shoulder. She hasn't cut her hair since being pregnant with Elizabeth and she likes its increasing weight.

"Excuse me while I instruct the children," Luke says, standing up.

"Luke picked up some supplies for Roman candles. A Lucero family recipe."

"I'm ready to be impressed," Bonnie says. Roy would not have approved of homemade fireworks. Bonnie doesn't really approve either, but Gus and Luke building Roman candles with their boys is better than Cheryl throwing Karly in the car with a box of sparklers.

Luke crouches in the group of boys. Karly, then Elizabeth, run over to see, five boys and two girls wide-eyed at the cardboard tube and glass jars full of powders.

If she were working, that would be the picture.

Gus watches the water, which is darkening into grays as the sun falls. This would have been another shot for herself. A good picture comes when someone is lost in thoughts, not empty of them, and the photographer has a connection to those thoughts. Either the photographer or the subject has to feel something about the other: it is one shot in a hundred for it to be both and a snapshot when it is neither. This was Bonnie's first sign that she and Roy were drifting apart: she stopped thinking, *that's the shot.*

"This place is going to be a monster," she says.

"The builders told me three stories tall."

"I wouldn't know what to do with so much."

She and Roy said similar things sitting on the Luceros' plot almost ten years ago. A few years before that, Bonnie and Roy built their place over a summer, one of the first structures on the east side of Red Bird Forest. They worked sunrise to sunset, discussing next steps during sandwich or coffee breaks, landing breathless on bedrolls over the dirt, then on a mattress, and finally on a mattress with a bedframe. As the walls and ceiling filled in around them, there was more to feel good about and less to say.

When the Luceros moved in two years later, their house had to be built nearer than expected to the Hadfords' because of the sloped plot, and it went up quick. They were close enough to hear each other at night if both houses left windows open, and Bonnie started making sure they did. She and Roy could breathe in the sounds of Gus and Annie making love until it was their sound, too.

One night after Annie died, Bonnie was alone in the bedroom and heard Gus crying. Maybe she should have left, but it felt important to listen, like her hearing might make it lighter for him to carry.

"Good sandwich," Gus says, then sips his beer.

Bonnie wonders if every now and then Gus sees Annie in town the way she does, in bodies that are not quite right: too thin, too short, the hair never black enough. Annie wore dresses made of fabrics bright and dull, patterned and plain, which Gus offered to Bonnie after. Bonnie took the box but donated the dresses the next day, knowing that if she kept them she would try them on and want them to fit.

The bus from Merrill passes by on the road on the other side of the water, a reminder of the rest of the world.

"The boys gonna eat?" Bonnie says.

"Sooner or later," Gus says.

Luke instructs the boys, his voice firm but too quiet for Bonnie to hear the details, and the girls come back for fresh sparklers. Elizabeth has also turned her T-shirt into a bikini top. Every time her daughter does what Karly does, Bonnie wants to stop her, but she needs to be patient. Elizabeth is building herself inside.

Bonnie suddenly misses her terribly, with a longing to hug her tightly, to squeeze her flat the way Cheryl does to Karly, or maybe to pull her growing shape onto her lap. She wants to hear one of her questions or statements that changes the world a tiny bit. Can pancakes be a birthday cake? Or, Tomorrow I had the best day. She is always confusing tomorrow and yesterday and today.

But Karly says, "Ta-da, now you're turned to stone," aiming her sparkler-wand at Elizabeth, and they run away.

"Ta-da now you're a princess," Elizabeth says to Karly, pointing it in the same way while running after her.

"Ta-da, now you're turned invisible."

A single pop echoes over the reservoir, someone shooting off a firework from across the water. It is almost dark enough to see it after hearing the sound.

"Can we now?" one of the boys yells. Luke kneels down and the kids gather around him.

Gus stares at the water: the sizzle, pop, arch into the sky, and the cheering from his sons and nephews, seems to happen outside of his head. He doesn't flinch.

Luke hands the tube to Ross. He takes a few steps back and lets Ross pack in mud, pour in something from two different jars ,and light the fuse dangling from the top of the tube. Ross holds the tube above his head with one hand and everyone listens to the sizzle and pop, then sees, so far away from them, the arch.

"Only Ross," Luke says. He watches his nephew do it again all by himself. The other kids stand on their toes to see into the tube. Ross bends over, stirring up the right strength of mud, a new fuse already dangling out of the tube.

Everyone looks up, waiting for the next burst of color, but Bonnie watches her daughter, standing next to Karly, both of their shirts down from their bikini tops. Karly jumps in place, up and down, up and down, but Elizabeth is still. The glow from the tube's sizzling light barely reaches Elizabeth's face until Ross holds the tube in the air, away from him like his uncle said, and the small explosion sets everything alight—then Elizabeth is gone, and there are yells, and Elizabeth is on the ground, curled, a tiny back, bodies moving around her, Luke telling them to clear away, give space, and Bonnie is already there.

She pulls her daughter onto her lap. Elizabeth's hands cover her eyes and she screams, screams, screams something over and over that Bonnie can't understand.

"Shh, sweetie, let's see," Bonnie says, hearing and seeing nothing but her daughter in her lap, the world a darkroom, the rest of life depending on what Elizabeth will expose from under her hands. Bonnie takes a breath that fills her body, letting it slow her heart so that the girl's heart, so close, might match a calmer, safer pace.

She carefully pulls Elizabeth's hands from her face: one eye is closed by a healthy lid, and the other is blood and swelling and screaming—

"I'm bringing a car," Gus says. Gus has come too, knows what to do.

"I felt it go by my ear," Karly says, squatting over Bonnie and Elizabeth. Bonnie surprises herself with how gently she asks Karly to step back, sweetie, stay back.

Elizabeth keeps screaming, and this time Bonnie hears it:

"I want my daddy," she screams. "I want my daddy."

Bonnie rocks her daughter on the dirt in the dark. The first firework of the town's show shoots off over the reservoir: a whistling arch explodes into red and white splinters that fall in a giant, drooping one-eyed stare.

# — Combustible Debris —

## 1987

"Hey girlie tiger, you ready to go to Ms. Camilla's?" Cheryl calls out to her grandbaby playing in the tall grass. She sits on the step to her trailer finishing the *Clayton Clamour* before work, skimming the photos on the back page of the winners from this year's Red Bird Mining Days competition. The morning is quiet, a clean June day that is cool enough for a jean jacket. Rain is coming and she is ready for it. Summer storms bring change, which is something she always needs even if it takes some convincing.

On the other side of the fence, she can hear the squeaking of chairs unfolding, a sound she knows from when she worked with a catering company. Last year they demolished the cabins that used to be on the other side of the fence and put in a row of identical, two-story homes the color of pancake batter. All six of the new homes have people in them who are new to Clayton. The *Clamour* article last week said the guy who built them lives in Merrill and calls the color "beach sand." Their second-story windows look into the trailer park but the blinds are always closed.

It was from last week's *Clamour* that she learned the same

developer made an offer to Mr. Campos, who owns the trailer park where Cheryl has lived for fifteen years. Why serve a single stack of pancakes when you could make it a double.

It only takes one cigarette to read the *Clamour*. Cheryl grabs the lighter from off the outdoor table then reaches behind her for the pack of cigarettes on the floor, taking at the same time the open can. Her whole adult life she's been learning how to not leave anything of hers sitting around open, not bottles or cups or cans. A good place to keep them when she's sitting on the top step to the trailer and the kids are outside is inside against the wall and on the floor.

There is nothing more about the offer for the trailer park in this week's paper. Every Friday, Cheryl sees Mr. Campos at the post office, and yesterday she got a petition ready to give to him today. It has eighteen signatures on it, at least one from each of the fourteen trailers. She got cute and had Karly sign, too, an orange smear made with a thick marker next to Cheryl's name for Trailer Seven. It begins, *To Mr. Campos: We have full lives in these trailers and we write to you now to save our home.* Cheryl wrote and rewrote the first line for days, but then got it down quickly yesterday after opening the pint of gin. Sometimes she doesn't think Mr. Campos would sell, but sometimes she does, and her mind spills into a future that looks like the past, moving from apartment to apartment with fewer belongings each time until it is just a duffel for her and one for the baby, only this time the baby would not be her daughter, Shannon, but her daughter's daughter, Karly.

She checks that the envelope is in her jacket pocket. She'd gone a month clean but now her head hurts and her mouth is dry. All day yesterday she knocked, waited, and if someone wasn't home she watched from her top step until they were. She only had that kind of patience when drinking, so she broke her streak. But this was different than other times: this was for keeping a place together.

She doesn't hear an answer from Karly. She leans over and sees grass wiggling which means Karly is just playing. Kids love the tall grass back there by the fence. Shannon used to build her own world in that grass, next to a fallen bookshelf that Mr. Campos eventually hauled away.

If it were coffee Cheryl was dying to drink right now, she'd pour herself a soup-bowl-full and hold it with both hands in the glorious outside morning. Instead, she reaches again for her can, takes the last sip, then folds it into the newspaper and puts the bundle on the floor. Since working at the post office, she's started reading the Merrill paper too, from the city down the canyon. That paper takes an average of two cigarettes. They have an international and a national news section, and she keeps waiting for California to come up. She's never cared for that state in the past, but her daughter took a trip out there at the beginning of the year and hasn't written home since April.

If Camilla doesn't get back soon to watch Karly, Cheryl will be late to work and might miss Mr. Campos, who always comes when they open. They don't like her taking Karly in, even though the post office is just down the street. When Shannon was little, Cheryl cleaned houses and just plopped the baby in the tub with a stuffie until it was time to clean the bathroom, then she'd plop her on a carpet somewhere. But now Cheryl is too tired for the hustle of cleaning gigs. She's too tired for anything but regular paychecks, benefits, someone to complain to when shit isn't right.

When Shannon comes back, they'll start the jewelry business in earnest: Crystals by Krane. Cheryl will make necklaces and earrings by commission after building a stock, and Shannon will keep the books. Shannon was always good at math. And she takes things more seriously than Cheryl does. When she finished high school, Shannon had the idea to make childcare a business in the trailer park. All fifteen years that Cheryl has lived there, women have been keeping an eye on each other's families, watching someone's kids for a few minutes or sometimes a few nights. But Shannon thought of looping in other kids from town and getting money involved. They had a good group going, but in the end the moms who needed it most couldn't pay. Cheryl sometimes worried certain moms would decide not to come back, the ones like Iris Pound, who had that look that any day she might decide that her body couldn't keep up.

Shannon had that look, too. She left on January first, after a night of staying at home so that Cheryl could go out. Cheryl heard her moving around early that day, heard her open the door and hold it closed so it wouldn't slam shut. Cheryl thought maybe Shannon had started seeing someone, and that maybe it could be a good guy, someone who could help Shannon out of feeling as stuck as her face always told Cheryl she was. But the note by the coffee maker, which hasn't been on since Shannon left, told Cheryl that Shannon was making herself unstuck. *Hi Mom,* it said. *I have to see CA. I'll write when I get there. I love you and K, S.* Cheryl was angry but not surprised when some of her jewelry was gone. Shannon, who has expensive taste, had stolen from her before.

One of the wishes Cheryl makes every day is for Shannon to know what it feels like to have words come out with a glow on them because of another person. For Cheryl, there'd been others since her baby's father, but no one else she'd loved like that, not in a way where the good parts were light enough to balance out the heavy of the bad. Even though the bad won in the end. But it wasn't like that for Shannon with her baby's daddy. Shannon never said who, but Cheryl guessed it was someone passing through, someone Shannon hasn't seen since.

"Hey girlie face, don't go too far," Cheryl calls into the grass. How different it is with a grandbaby. She doesn't get the flapping in her heart that happened every time Shannon wandered off when she started walking. It could be that it isn't Cheryl who's changed, but the baby. Karly is curious and wild as her mom, but already she shows more loyalty. Last week, Cheryl set up her jewelry table, thin wires, tiny clasps, and a dozen stones separated into boxes; when she came back from the bathroom, the tray was flipped over, metal studding the floor. Karly tried to help clean up, her pudgy fingers grasping at the tiny pieces, some as small as glitter. Cheryl has never seen Shannon clean up her own mess.

*What a beautiful yard!*

*I thought we could start out here until the sun gets too high.*

*And you've set out chairs!*

Cheryl can hear but not see a group of women on the other side of the tall wooden fence.

*Did everyone finish the book?*

*You chose it, you should start.*

*Did you plant these from seed?*

Karly stumbles over from the tall grass, bare feet on the dirt, and starts smacking the table's post. Cheryl puts out the cigarette in the empty can and stands. She has one last full one in the back of the fridge, blocked by the big jar of pickles, for emergencies. Define emergency.

Karly reaches for a lighter on the table or maybe the hotdogs next to it. Cheryl has been dressing Karly in hand-me-downs from other trailers, and every now and then something she didn't give away of Shannon's. Today she's wearing a T-shirt built for a seven-year-old, like a dress. She is in the motion phase when they figure out how to move and can't stop.

"Not yet," Cheryl says, swatting Karly's hand. Cheryl left the hotdogs out to remember to give them to Camilla for Karly's lunch. Someone said you could eat them raw, which kids know by instinct. Shannon used to beg to eat anything raw, even bacon, peeling slices out of the package like American cheese if no one caught her. But in Shannon's last letter, arrived more than two months ago, she said she'd found the "vegan" lifestyle. What the hell, Shannon could be a vegan right here in Clayton, Colorado, taking care of her own daughter and her aging mother. Though Cheryl looks pretty good for a grandma a calendar's page away from forty-five.

"Up, up, up!" Karly says.

*Should we start with the end?*

*You always do that!*

"Up, up, up!" Karly smacks Cheryl's thighs. Cheryl leans down to her and her necklace swings. Karly reaches for it and almost gets it. Cheryl tucks into her shirt the turquoise pendant, one of her only pieces she didn't make herself. A pendant against co-dependence, he said, the man who gave it to her. What a dumbass. Him, too, but mostly Cheryl.

*I was disappointed she went back to him.*

*You always are.*

*She goes right back to women's work: he's blind and his house burns down? Now she's a nurse.*

*For his pride.*

*But they're meant to be together, the whole book drives toward it.*

Karly is in Cheryl's lap when Camilla sings out, "Sorry, sorry!" rushing around the corner. She wears a scarf over a T-shirt and her hundred tiny braids are up in a bun. "My car wouldn't start. I got back as fast as I could."

"Are you okay? From where?" The sun moves an inch and now reaches however jillions of miles onto Cheryl's face. Cheryl feels annoyed that Camilla is late, guilty for asking her, again, to watch Karly, nervous about the petition and Mr. Campos and the trailer park, yearning for her daughter, and overheated. Lately she never feels one thing at a time.

"Up at the elementary school. I had an interview but probably didn't get it."

Camilla is ten years younger than Cheryl and in the five

years since she moved into the trailer park, she's worked more jobs than Cheryl can track. Camilla thinks people don't trust her because she's Black; Cheryl always tells her to have those dumbasses call her for the best reference they've ever heard, but Camilla never takes her up on it. The last time Cheryl offered, she realized Camilla knows most people in town don't trust Cheryl, either.

"And you ran all the way down? You—"

"Aren't you late for work? Come here, Karly baby, let's see what flowers we can pick."

Cheryl can't stop herself from going back to the fridge and reaching for the emergency can. Her whole body feels warm and it gives her an urge to cry, something she almost never does. Not many people would run down a mountain to keep a deal with her. For every job Camilla can't keep, she's helped Cheryl half a dozen times. The accumulation of it is a volume greater than what Cheryl could drink. She pops open the can and chugs, crouching on the ground in the cold of the fridge.

When she stands back on the step, she can see over the fence. The group of women are gone but a circle of chairs remains, a book tented on each seat.

There used to be trees back there, giant spruce with thick trunks in front of each cabin. For a few days, the cabins were down but the trees still up, just like the story a guy at a casino once told Cheryl about a fire in the suburbs that ate house after house but left the trees standing. For a while, Cheryl thought maybe the workers had gone on strike, refusing to destroy what was ancient and sacred, but it turned out they were waiting on some detail in the contract with Vander Troy, a local man who made a business of taking away trees.

On the trailer park side of the fence, Camilla points out a columbine and tells Karly to never ever pick it, that it is there for everyone.

Cheryl would drink one more if she had it.

*

At the post office, Roy Hadford is nowhere to be seen. He has been working with Cheryl for a year and still doesn't unlock the doors for the customers when she is late.

On the other side of the door, waiting to come in, is Bradley Kind, a fifty-year-old ex-cowboy who still wears the hat.

"Morning, Brad," Cheryl says, unlocking and then pushing open the door. He does the one-handed man-wave and turns toward his PO box. He got drunk as a skunk at the Inn a few months ago and made some persistent moves on Cheryl—she is over it, but he hasn't looked her in the eye since.

The backdoor to the sorting room slams.

"Hey, Roy," she calls out. "Did ya forget to let the customers in?"

It is her job to unlock the doors, but she can say anything to Roy without getting a reaction. Sometimes she gets him to talk, but the factors have to be lined up right: they have to be outside, he has to have something to do with his hands, and there can't be anyone else there to listen. It happens most when she is on a cigarette break and he is shoveling snow or hammering something into something else.

Roy waves without answering and picks up the first packet of mailers, the ad for the liquor store in Merrill. That place has aisles and aisles of stuff most people in Clayton have never heard of unless they've studied the flyer. Cheryl sometimes wanders down the rows, hoping no one will see her already breaking promises to herself by going in. She does that in High Spirits, the place in Clayton, too, but only when it's Mr. Ji at the counter and not his wife. Mrs. Ji watches her like she already knows Cheryl's breaking a rule, a fact that makes her likely to break another.

Roy pops the string and starts dealing flyers like cards.

"We're low on stamps," she calls out.

Roy puts a hand in the air without stopping with the flyers, which means he heard about the stamps and will order more before they run out, and that they'll arrive exactly when she's decided he forgot so that later she will feel bad for doubting him. Anyone eavesdropping on them wouldn't know it, but Cheryl and Roy are a perfect team.

She crouches down to unlock the safe kept under the register, her pendant clanking against the metal.

"Do you think anyone's ever held up a post office?" she says, lifting up the cash drawer. She's said it before and will keep saying it until he comes up with a reply. He pops the next bunch of mailers, a bright green announcement that Mountain Foods is under new ownership and is now Mountain Mart, and starts the second layer that will be curled into a tube and shoved into PO boxes and mailboxes, then tossed into whatever folks use to hold their kindling.

"Hey Roy, if I'm ever in the back and Mr. Campos comes in, come get me, okay?"

"Sure," Roy says. A small victory for Cheryl. Next thing you know, they'll be inviting each other over for Thanksgiving. Roy and his wife have a girl the same age as Karly, but you'd never learn about her from Roy.

She pulls over the rolling bin holding the delivery from Merrill. They are supposed to sort the letters before the junk flyers, but that is another wordless agreement she and Roy have: Roy gives the letter bin a six-foot radius like it is full of used diapers, leaving it for Cheryl to sort between helping customers. Learning private details about her neighbors is a perk of working at the post office. But one thing about Cheryl is that she doesn't tell.

In her first handful of letters, there it is:

*Ms. Cheryl Krane.*

No return address, but Cheryl knows her daughter's writing. She has kept her *y*'s floppy like that since grade school, looped all over the place like dangling jewels. Cheryl opens it quickly to find another envelope, just like she taught Shannon: always use two envelopes, unless you want someone in the mailroom, like Cheryl, learning your business. The front door opens with its ding and Cheryl puts the unmarked envelope in her pocket.

"It's you, Mr. Campos!" she says. He carries two thick manila envelopes and wears a sweater vest. His hair and mustache, newly excavated from a beard, are neatly trimmed. She puts his first envelope on the scale. The calm from her two cans has worn off and now she isn't sure how to give a landlord of a trailer park a petition that asks him not to sell a trailer park.

"Expedited or regular?" she says. "I like the new 'stache."

"Regular," he says, handing her the next envelope, maybe smiling a little. "Stamps too, please." He was Shannon's high school history teacher. Cheryl might have worried that Mr. Campos failed Shannon because of how many times they were late with rent, except that history wasn't the only class that Shannon failed.

"One book? Two? We got birds, boats, or flags."

Cheryl knows he will pick flags, but it's polite to ask—he points at flags and lifts one finger.

"We have something for you," she says. She grabs the envelope from her jean jacket and hands it to him with the stamps. "It's all of them, all of us, and we can meet with you later if you want."

"To what does this refer?" He looks down at her, so she stands, but he's still a foot taller.

Cheryl grabs her pendant. "Or we can also set up a meeting, if you want, to talk about it more. I could come see the museum and meet you." This sounds flirtatious because the museum hasn't opened to the public yet. But it is instinct, not intent.

"But what—"

"It's about what was in the paper last week." Cheryl cuts him off—she can't help it when she's nervous. "Just read it when you can and let us know what you think." She smiles bigger than she feels like smiling, which she does when she feels small and easy to blow away. Mr. Campos sees this smile every time she is late with rent.

"Goodbye, then," he says, which is what he says every time Cheryl is late with rent.

He walks away, holding the envelope casually, without tearing into it with curiosity or wonder or need, a willpower Cheryl has never had.

Cheryl pulls out the envelope from Shannon and looks at it on the table, imagining she could be like Mr. Campos and open it at home, at night, after Karly has gone to bed. She rubs her pendant and hopes: say you're coming home.

She opens the envelope: *To Mr. Campos: We have full lives in these trailers and we write to you now to save our home.*

She rushes out to the empty parking lot but Mr. Campos is nowhere. She starts running toward the reservoir and the trail that will take her to the museum, the brand new building that Mr. Campos is filling with people's memories, which is where he must have gone because she wouldn't know where else to look. She runs in the middle of the dirt road and the clouds have darkened the day and the smell of rain coming fills her lungs and limbs. She runs and her pendant bounces off the buttons on her jacket making tiny clacks counting down until the first crack of thunder followed by a stab of lightning, the world telling Cheryl to turn back. Twenty years ago, she would not have listened, she would have kept running and running; it was not until fifteen years ago when Shannon was eight or nine, that Cheryl started to stop and listen. It was raining with the sky this dark but in the early morning, 8:09 on the dashboard of that guy's truck, a rare morning rain. Cheryl had asked Erika, who used to live in Number One, to watch Shannon for two nights so she could go to the casinos in Silver City with what's-his-name, and it was halfway through the third night when Cheryl snapped out of it, waking up in the hotel bathroom and pissing that guy off by making him take her back—and when she finally got home, in the heavy, strange morning rain, the door was hanging wide open and Shannon sat on the top step with three boxes of cereal around her in a hungry heap, and said, "Ms. Erika told me to keep it open so she could hear if I needed anything." The feeling that open door gave Cheryl, like she had started something that would be too big for her to stop, helped her do better for a long time after that.

But now she stops running only fifty yards from the trailer park and the new pancake-batter homes behind it, where Karly is learning about columbines. When the smell of rain turns to water in heavy, distinct drops, she knows: now it is Shannon's turn to run and run.

Cheryl breathes in what the world tells her. Shannon is not coming back.

The sky breaks open and the rain falls hard. Cheryl crosses her arms over the petition between her jean jacket and her heart, keeping what is important as dry as she can.

# — Mitigation —

## 1994

Jackie is on her way to buy heart candy when she sees Patrick's clean black Lexus among the dirty dented Subarus in the Mountain Mart parking lot. She stops in the middle of the road she is crossing, turns, and takes the first back road she comes to.

Maybe it isn't his car. It would be a two-hour drive for him from Denver, and he doesn't have snow tires. He didn't have snow tires. She didn't get close enough to see if the Lexus in the parking lot has snow tires, and if it does, if they are new.

In her office in an elementary school two miles up the icy dirt road, a letter she received on Friday sits on her desk. It has been there over the weekend, in a red envelope, unopened.

To: Jackie Hoyt
Fire Mitigation and Public Outreach Office
P.O. Box 2421
Clayton, CO 80477

There is no return name or address on the envelope, but it is Patrick's handwriting. The same sharp *k*'s and small *o*'s she used to find on notes in her purse and taped to her bathroom mirror. She doesn't know how he got the address.

Does the letter tell her he is coming? That he misses her? That he is thinking about last Valentine's Day, which was a long Sunday of Jackie waiting for Patrick, wondering what he would do, when he would do it, how. He'd ended up tapping on her window, late, in the dark, with flowers, after his family had gone to bed.

For the first time in the six weeks she's lived in Clayton, she feels hot. A fever burns out of the slices of air between her mittens and jacket and her pant cuffs and boots with no tread. She pulls her layers apart, undoing what her landlord-roommate, Mae Ji, taught her to do for winter in the mountains. The heat from her body spills into the cold.

She turns to look back down the road. It is quiet.

If that is his car in the parking lot, would he show up at her office? Is he driving around town checking signs on buildings? The PO box number protects her, and he would never guess that her office is tucked in the corner of an elementary school—but Clayton is small enough to find someone if you want to.

She could go back to her rented room. Mae is home today. She could tell Mae that she doesn't want Patrick to find her. The tag on Mae's parka says Child's Large, but Mae would stand up to anyone. Jackie and Mae are about the same age, but Mae already has a house to rent and a place in the world. She works on a ranch and spends her weekends outside splitting and stacking firewood, patching the roof, or taming the drifts of snow that would block the front door if she let them. Her parents used to own the liquor store in town, and she worked there since she was little and through high school, learning how to deal with drunks and liars. Mae would know how to not let someone like Patrick in.

But it is probably safest at the elementary school. The kids from the after-school program and their counselor, Allen, will make Jackie feel better. Mae and Allen are dating, and sometimes Allen walks home with Jackie to visit Mae. He smells like coffee, natural soap, and thick winter clothes, has a long blond braid, and wears moccasins even in the snow. He says things like "Let it heal," when one of the kids he supervises does something mean to another.

If Allen stays over, sometimes in the morning while making coffee Jackie watches Mae and Allen sit on the porch in their jackets. Allen usually has his feet up, Mae usually smokes, and Allen's dog, Freyda, runs up and down the road. They never hold hands or rub each other's shoulders, and when he is not there, Mae never pines for him to call or write or visit. Jackie wonders if she could be like that, too, if she had someone like Allen.

Before taking the last turn to Clayton Elementary School, she hears humming. A man crouches in the snow next to a snowman, which is lumpy in bottom, middle, and top. The man wears thick flannel, boots, and a beard.

"Daddy, Mommy said we don't have carrot only potato!" A little girl with an armful of clothes and a potato shuffles toward him in loud snow pants. A scarf trails in the snow behind her.

Jackie slips and catches herself before falling all the way.


Though everyone she asks denies it, Jackie suspects that the Colorado Mountain Fire Mitigation and Public Outreach intern office, Clayton location, used to be a broom closet. She has a taped sign on the door (Hours: M-TH 3-7), one wooden desk that is currently buried in hate mail thanks to the forum two weeks ago, one wooden chair, and no windows. Her only decoration is a new 1993 Merrill County map, thickly laminated, stamped with the US Forest Service official seal, and webbed with latitude and longitude. A shaky oval targets the southeast corner, drawn with dry-erase marker and labeled "Red Bird

Forest" in Jackie's neat letters. In the lower right corner, a visiting kid used a Sharpie to leave thick confident strokes: Hi.

The red envelope without a return address glows among the others, which are mostly white and tan. She props it against the wall, debating: if she opens it and it tells her where to meet him, or where to meet him at a time that has already passed, he might still be there waiting. And if she goes to see if he is still there, she might snap like dry wood in a wind storm and he might pick up and then keep the pieces.

Something thunks. Snow slides slowly down the window of the emergency exit door across the hall. The emergency exit doesn't alarm like it warns it will, but it locks from the outside, which means that kids in the after-school program often sneak out then need to be let back in. In Jackie's first week of work, the after-school kids learned that Jackie is the kind of adult who doesn't tell when they sneak out and who lets them in when they tap on the door. Two fourth-grade girls, Karly and Elizabeth, are out there now, in the darkening afternoon and air dropped to single digits. They wear T-shirts and pack snowballs with bare hands to throw straight up and catch on the way down, or to aim at trees, windows, emergency exits. They look like sisters, their hair tangled and long.

Another thunk. When Jackie walks up to the door to see if they want in, the girls wave and run. Elizabeth wears large glasses like the ones that Patrick's daughter wears; Jackie has never met Patrick's daughter, or her twin sister, or Patrick's wife. She's seen their pictures without him knowing, flipping through the photos in his wallet while he showered.

She waves back even though the girls have already disappeared into the parking lot. The outdoor lights flick on, down-pointing flares in the gray.

She grabs one of the letters in a white envelope, the red envelope burning in the corner of her eye. She already knows the gist of what the letter in the white envelope will say: cancel the prescribed burn in Red Bird Forest because X. Red Bird Forest, sixty-five acres of county land on the south end of town, serves a dozen different purposes, depending on who you ask. People say it is for 4X4s and BB guns, others say quiet and solitude; for snowshoeing, not for dogs; for dogs especially. Someone told her that a decade ago, some sweet but misinformed teacher brought a group of kids out to Red Bird Forest to plant new trees, which explains the high fuel load.

The forest extends down to a park and part of the remaining headframe of the Red Bird mine and the Clayton Mining Museum. A few years ago, the headframe and museum caught fire. There are rumors that it was arson and that the man who managed the museum, a high school history teacher, went nuts afterwards. When Jackie asked Allen about it, he said that sometimes people in Clayton need a story, but then he didn't offer another one. The headframe still sits there, charred and broken, waiting for someone in an office to make a decision.

When the Forest Service team came for their site visit, Jackie could see as easily as they did that if anything happened within a hundred yards of those dried out pines, the area would combust. At the town hall meeting two weeks ago, squeezed between the announcement of a new bus stop near the post office and a committee trying to allow boating on the reservoir, her proposal for a prescribed burn roused the sleepy audience: You can't just do that. We should get a vote on it. My grandparents camped in those woods. We got kids camping in Red Bird, where would they go? How's it healthier if it's burnt up? What if it catches wind and sets the whole town on fire?

After the paper published an article about the proposal, people have been calling every day. They call her "office number," reaching a wall phone by the after-school program parent check-in table in the school cafeteria. They call to tell her why a prescribed burn is not the answer. While listening to people's concerns, she watches Allen and his assistant, Lonna, wipe noses and pass around bowls of goldfish.

The letter in the white envelope is on thick stationary with beautiful handwriting.

Mrs. Hoyt,
Our family has lived by Red Bird Woods since World War II, when my father built our home after serving our country. My husband and I put up the bird houses around the east end—have you seen them? If you burn the woods what will happen to the birds and where could I send my father to rest?

Please consider, with God,
Rachel Kyles

She grabs another letter and works its seal, staring at the *Clayton Clamour* from last week, opened to the full page near the back with the headline "Prescribed Burn Proposal Sets Fire to Town Hall" and a picture of Jackie standing in the middle of the rabble afterwards, holding up her notebook and a pen like an amateur detective. She wore a sweater that Patrick had given her, not because she missed him, but because it is a beautiful sweater—wool, warm, and deep green. Since living in the mountains, she has been asking more of her clothes, pulling sweaters over her hands, up her neck, and into her pants, and that sweater is the only one that still fits her right.

Is that how Patrick found her? Had he been scanning newspapers of small towns, knowing she didn't have the guts to go too far? She knew the lady who took the pictures at the forum: it was the mother of Elizabeth, the girl outside with the large glasses. She was not asked for permission to use the photo, and if she had been, Jackie would have said no. She barely recognizes herself in the picture, but Patrick would. The timing worked out: he could have seen the photo and sent her a letter asking to meet on Valentine's Day at a time and place she's supposed to know about by now.

This second letter from a white envelope is on torn-out notebook paper:

Hi. Please do not start a fire on Red Bird. I live right next to it and what if my house burns down too. I would expect full compensation and even that wouldn't fix what can't be replaced. What if it was your house.

She tosses it onto the other side of the desk. She came to Clayton to disappear, but instead she's become more recognizable than she's ever been. Over the weekend, she was even approached at Annie's Café, where for the last month she's been sipping hot chocolate and eavesdropping on soft-spoken regulars talk about how to get squirrels off the bird feeders. When she walked in yesterday morning someone said, "Aren't you the Red Bird fire lady?"

She hears footsteps in the hall.

"Missus?"

It is Ashlynn, one of her favorite after-school program kids.

"Hey kiddo, Happy Valentine's Day," Jackie says. She doesn't have the bag of chocolate hearts she hoped to get at the store earlier, so she holds out a bag of dessert mints from her bottom drawer, a secret stash that most kids know about and some kids steal from. Tall and big with straight black hair, Ashlynn is a few years older than the other kids in the program, and she never plays with any of them. Ashlynn's mom is Lonna, Allen's assistant.

Ashlynn mumbles something with mints in her mouth and hands Jackie today's mail, more letters. She wears a baggy white

T-shirt with giant pink bows stuck to it like butterflies trapped in glue. One of them dangles at the spot of her belly button, a broken wing held on by a thread.

"What, hon?"

"The phone's for you," Ashlynn says.

Jackie feels hot again, the way she overheated on her walk up. She takes off her scarf, pink for Valentine's Day. It could be Patrick. He could be calling from the same phone booth outside of the Mountain Mart that Jackie uses because Mae's place doesn't have a phone. Jackie stands in that booth once a week to call her sister, watching people walk across the parking lot, smelling the wet, cold wooden walls. Her sister doesn't know Patrick's name, only that Jackie acts like she has a broken heart.

Maybe Patrick's elbows are up on the same wooden ledge where Jackie puts hers, fit into the same dips from a decade of other people making calls. Maybe he is tracing the initials that teenagers or distraught adults carved into the wood with coins or pocketknives or pens.

She puts a mint in her mouth, hoping it will cool her down. "Thanks, I'm coming," she says to Ashlynn. She grabs the red envelope with her name and address written in Patrick's k's and o's. If he found this number then he might come to the building; if he does, she wants to show him she didn't open the letter, to prove that she wouldn't.

"Did you wear pink for Valentine's Day?" she says to Ashlynn, grateful that the girl walks slowly.

"I don't know," Ashlynn says. She is painfully soft-spoken. One of those kids who makes Jackie want a volume knob on her arm.

When they get to the cafeteria, Ashlynn goes to the far corner by the coat rack and cubbies, where her mom chats over a child with a parent, who tries to put a hat on his kid's dodging head. The parent wears the chunky, worn Sorels that most Clayton adults wear, clumps of snow clinging to the lining like small animals. Jackie identifies parents by their jackets, most of which are from the eighties: puffy, synthetic, and patched over in spots where someone sat too close to a fire.

Most of the after-school kids cram into one of the fold-down bench tables. Allen, his legs too long, has a chair pulled up to one end with his back to her. He wears flannel in gray and red. Freyda sits at his feet. Kids' skinny arms reach near him like swaying branches, coming away with small leaves of construction paper.

She picks up the phone, supine on the table by the sign-out clipboard.

"This is the Fire Mitigation and Public Outreach Office, how can I help you?"

Silence.

"Hello?"

Her body heats again, in one rush toward her head. The wide, bright elementary school cafeteria deflates into a cave, in which sounds and colors echo.

"I'm sorry, I can't hear you."

*Look, a heart!* a boy at the table from the depths of the cave says. He holds up the shape of a mummy.

*I'm making one for my dog*, a girl says.

*And maybe one for your mom, too*, Allen says.

She tries to sound professional, but it is Patrick. This is a game they used to play: Jackie would wait days for him to call, sitting on her couch in her apartment and watching her phone on the counter, making herself leave so that she could rush back in and see if a light blinked on the answering machine. He never said anything on the message so that there couldn't be anything to keep: a silent message said he was coming over later.

She can smell him through the phone, his body always sharp with cologne, a scent that must be cutting through the soft wood of the phone booth at the Mountain Mart. She watches Allen fold construction paper then draw hook after hook while kids follow the lines with thick, safe scissors.

"I'm hanging up," she says, then waits. Three, two, one. She presses the telephone hook.

"Jackie!" The kids spot her. Allen turns and waves with them. She wants to jump into the cave, squeeze into the table between children who know nothing about Patrick. Make a card, get buried in glitter and sequins and tell someone she loves them. Her sister, her sister's kids. Allen and Mae.

Jackie waves and releases the telephone hook but keeps the phone at her ear, letting the hum of the dial tone pour in.

She'd been looking for a way to leave Denver since September, the month she first started stealing time with the photos in Patrick's wallet. When the director of Jackie's master's program in land management offered her the Clayton internship last November, to start in January, she didn't tell Patrick. For the first weeks after her move, she wondered if flowers arrived at her empty apartment in Denver, if the phone rang against its naked walls. She hoped that after six months in the mountains, the life she'd ended up with in Denver would be struck by lightning and all that was dead and dry would go up in flames and she could start again.

Around the craft table, paper hearts unfold in red, white, and pink.

"Mrs. Jackie!" Lonna calls across the cafeteria, pulling Ashlynn up from the floor where she was coloring. Lonna is half the thickness of her daughter, bleached blond and with tough skin, as if she's fallen asleep often in a tanning booth.

"Vander's wanting to talk to you again, asked me to grab you before you left," she calls out, walking toward her. She nudges Ashlynn to the craft table and comes for Jackie. "He's coming in an hour to pick me and Ashy up. You'll still be here?"

Jackie holds up a finger, pretending to listen closely to someone on the phone. Vander, Lonna's brother, is Vander Troy of Troy's Trees. He slipped in at the end of the forum, his thick, brown coat the same color as his beard. When he approached Jackie afterwards, he shook her hand and talked at her the way that confident men with money always do. Just let me take the wood, he said; you can set the stumps on fire if you want to. He handed her a business card. *Troy's Trees: The Answer is Clear-Cut.*

The phone starts beeping and Jackie hangs up quickly.

"Happy Valentine's Day!" The kids sing out to her.

"Happy Valentine's Day!" she tries to sing back. Her chest is airy and full of fluttering pieces of paper. She starts toward the cafeteria kitchen.

"Allen?" she says. "Can I use the back phone?" He turns, looks at her, and nods. His eyes are brown and kind and deep, which is something he and Mae have in common, their way of looking at you and knowing.

Mae and Allen must have the kind of secret that Jackie thought she had with Patrick, secret because it is strong.

She walks slowly, or maybe it only feels slow, with the kids laughing and gluing their own hands together on Valentine's Day behind her, Lonna hovering to the side, and the kitchen getting closer and closer until she is inside its boundary that smells of canned green beans and the metal of the counter where each day children slide tray after tray down the line. She is behind the counter, beyond the industrial fridges, and enters the break room, where every day the kitchen staff, then Allen and Lonna, share a desk and a chair that is identical to the one in Jackie's office. But they have a giant window that looks out to the parking lot. They can see who is coming and when.

She sits, moves Lonna's purse and Allen's cloth bag of trail mix to the side, pulls the phone closer, and dials. She knows his home number by heart even though this is only the second time calling it. She used to say the numbers out loud to herself when she wanted to dial them.

She listens to the rings. If his wife is there, Jackie will tell her.

Not everything, but enough to get the debris out of her lungs that makes it hard to breathe, a problem that doesn't come from the altitude like everyone says.

She doesn't know how she will say it.

Three rings. Four.

"Hello?" It is a woman. It must be the woman with the short curly hair in the wallet photograph. She must be sitting alone on Valentine's Day, believing in some world that hasn't been since Jackie and Patrick met two Novembers ago. Jackie worked at a hardware store and Patrick came looking for outdoor Christmas lights, then for hooks to put them on his home, then for her.

"Hello?" his wife says again. Two other voices sing in the background and through the window two girls, Karly and Elizabeth, emerge from around the corner of the building. Karly's arms swing through the dusk, but Elizabeth's arms are under her shirt like they have frozen to her skin. They see Jackie, back-lit through the cafeteria office window, and Karly bends down to mold a snowball. The girls through the phone continue their song, something rhyming and silly that projects over the girls outside.

"Anyone there?" Patrick's wife says.

Headlights entering the parking lot spotlight the girls, then turn. Jackie stands up to see if the car is a black Lexus, but the window explodes from Karly's snowball.

And then she hears the voice she hasn't heard since just after Christmas when he called to say he couldn't visit, after all, not until the holidays were over—

"Who is it?" Patrick says through the phone. Behind the window blotted with snow, Elizabeth's mom, the photographer who'd taken the picture of Jackie in the green sweater that was a gift from this man on the phone, gets out of her car.

"Just hang up," he says to his wife, but Jackie does it first.

She opens the red envelope. On green construction paper and folded into one thousand folds, it says:

To Fire Lady: I play in the woods. I like to run. I like to see animals. Please don't burn them. From, Shawn O.

Outside, Elizabeth's mom in a thick red sweater stands with the girls and the girls point at Jackie through the window. Elizabeth's mom waves and Jackie pretends to be busy writing something down and the two girls run away, this time toward the front entrance, where it is now safe for them to return and reveal that they snuck outside since they are going home.

Jackie can see by their wild hair, stiff from the cold, by Karly's arms, pale from the thin air but resisting, that they will not grow up to be women who are lost in time and space. They will not be women who never learned how to orient themselves by the rings of trees or the circles of light in parking lots at night. They will learn how to light the world around them on fire without getting burned.

# — Fuel Density —

## 2002

When Ross Lucero was twelve, he won the Clayton, Colorado Red Bird Miners Day hand-mucking competition for kids twelve and under. An eleven-year-old girl named Crystal Troy almost beat him. It took Crystal eight minutes and fifty-four seconds to shovel dirt into a wagon up to the line, push the wagon down a fifteen-foot segment of railroad track and tip it over at the end. It took Ross eight minutes and forty seconds, which won him fifty bucks and his picture in the paper. His neighbor, Bonnie Hadford, took a picture and gave his dad a framed copy to hang on the wall.

Two months later was the Fourth of July that Ross did something wrong with a homemade Roman candle and it backfired into Bonnie's daughter's face, leaving a six-year-old girl what they call "legally blind" in the right eye. He would have given back the fifty-dollar bill, the framed photo, the feeling he got when his dad squeezed his arm to congratulate him, to have never lit that fuse.

Ross has not gone to Red Bird Days since the year he won, until now. This is the event's thirty-year anniversary and the prizes are higher to celebrate. Red Bird Park is packed with tourists and competitors, some of them from out of state. People are taking short hikes into the forest, watching their kids on the play structures in the gravel pit, taking photos of the plaque on the fence that surrounds the pile of charred wood that used to be the headframe of the Red Bird Mine, and buying bowls of chili, T-shirts, and locally-made jewelry. This kind of a crowd makes Clayton feel like somewhere else.

Ross writes his name on the sign-up sheet for adult hand mucking: *R. Lucero,* and, to the right, his age, *23.* He scans the sheet and sees that he is the youngest to enter men's hand mucking ages twenty-one and up. First prize is five hundred dollars, the same price his family charges for delivering and stacking three cords of wood. He's chosen hand mucking because it is the only event he might win. He's doing this for the money.

Ross has become the strongest person he knows in terms of muscle. He realized this one day last September when his dad, who used to be the strongest person he knew, wanted to quit four-fifths of the way through a job and wait for the next day. Ross finished the job on his own and could have done more. All it took was focus: keep the mind empty and the body in motion. Feed your thoughts and feelings to your muscles. Ross has endless material to feed to his muscles because his mind is always full of things that don't exist anywhere else: a girlfriend, a truck with working windows, his mother, Elizabeth Hadford with two working eyes. He has gone over those five seconds with the Roman candle again and again. In his mind, when he packs the end of the tube with mud, pours the powders in, first from the big jar, then the small, and lights the fuse, he holds the tube up high so that the bottom aims at his face, not at the little girl to his right.

"A kid with guns like yours should go for the gold." Vander Troy stands next to Ross, both of them watching hand mucking. "Double jack gives a thousand bucks each this year, you know that, right?"

Double jack needs skills Ross doesn't have. He grew up chopping wood, which means he has the stamina and his swing has enough force, but he doesn't have the precision to hit the head of a steel nail as small as a quarter. More than that, double jack drillers work in teams of two, one guy swinging the hammer and the other holding the nail and spinning it between every hit; Ross doesn't have the trust.

"Five hundred dollars for hand mucking is better than zero for losing double jack," Ross says.

Vander laughs loudly, which Ross has been hearing a lot of lately. For forever in Clayton it has been Lucero firewood or Troy firewood, and now Gus, Ross, and Ross's seventeen year-old brother, Tyler, are moving to Scottsbluff, Nebraska. Vander has been to the Lucero place often this month, thinking about buying the wood splitter, the shed full of saws, the old pickup, talking through their goods and bads. When Ross was sixteen, he fixed up and moved into the garage, from where he has been hearing all that his dad and Vander say.

Two teens lift the wagon up from its tilt so that the next competitor can fill it with the same dirt and push in the opposite direction. It was Vander's niece, Crystal, who almost beat Ross eleven years ago. A few years later, Crystal got pregnant and dropped out of high school. Ross doesn't know where she went after that.

"Still can't believe you boys are taking off at a time like this," Vander says. "I'm not complaining, but hell." In March, Merrill County and the US Forest Service announced a plan they said would mitigate forest fires near cities and towns by decreasing fuel density, an alternative to the prescribed burn that residents keep voting out. Forests within a five-mile radius to any town will be thinned to a density of less than ten tons per acre to prevent quick spread, using local labor when possible. Gus and Vander met with guys from the county and learned that not only would the county pay for the labor, but whoever did the thinning could keep—and sell—the wood. It would have been the busiest they'd ever been with more than twice the pay. But by the time they found this out, someone from California had bought the Luceros' house. It would all be left to the Troys.

"You'll keep up," Ross says. The Troys cut differently from the Luceros. The Troys have half a dozen employees, high school kids they barely pay, and deal with builders from Merrill who need large plots cleared fast. The Luceros just have Gus, Ross, and sometimes Tyler, so they take the small sites the Troys won't bother with, like when the Sonbergs wanted a horse arena, when the Olsons expanded their driveway. Ross never liked those bigger jobs working for developers. His dad had taken a few of them, always from some guy across the country telling them what to do over the phone. Even if it is a perfect site for cutting, easy access for the truck, a slope that isn't too steep, that kind of work leaves a different smell in the air, like it's you versus the land instead of you working with it.

"Why you all moving on, anyway? I can't get sense of it from your dad," Vander says.

They are moving to Scottsbluff to help Grandma, Gus's mother who lives in the same house where she raised her boys and who is starting to forget which meal it is. They are moving to help Gus's brother, Luke, save his concrete business. They are moving because Gus can't work the way he used to, and no matter how hard Ross pushes himself, they both know—though never say—that he can't keep the same pace by himself.

"Family," Ross says.

The idea has been on the table for a decade, but it was Ross who brought it up in earnest last fall. He had just gotten home from his first call for the Merrill County volunteer fire department, a kitchen fire in a breakfast restaurant that had been contained by the time Ross got down the canyon. He felt foolish for rushing down there for nothing and for how much he hoped that a certain other volunteer, who lived on the east side of Merrill, might have been called, too. Foolish for thinking on every minute of the thirty-minute drive down the canyon that they might have been driving toward each other.

When he got home, he felt foolish for his life in Clayton. *Luke still need help in concrete?* he'd said to his dad, who had just rinsed out his coffee mug, a tool that no one had ever seen him wash.

"Family's the only reason I'd believe," Vander says.

"Next up in hand mucking, Amanda Fuller from Casper, Wyoming," a man calls through a megaphone. They stagger men and women muckers with the same wagon and track, but with separate prize categories. Ross is three after Amanda, the last to compete in men's.

"Two…one…muck!"

"Dang, girl, bend at the knees," Vander says. Ross should laugh to be polite, but he can never pull that off.

"Be back in a bit," Ross says. He looks Vander in the eye like his dad taught him.

"You can probably take your time waiting on this gal." Vander rummages in his front pocket and pulls out a toothpick.

Ross wanders into the park, trying not to look for Collin, the other volunteer firefighter who Ross thought might have been on the call months ago. When they finished orientation and training in August, they went to a pool hall in Merrill to celebrate, a volunteer fire department tradition. Ross and Collin stayed at the bar while everyone else circled tables with pool sticks, sharing pitchers. Ross took two hours to get through one beer, the whole time pushing back on a pull to say more to Collin, to not look disappointed when Collin left for the bathroom or to fill in at a pool table or once to smoke a cigarette, something he didn't say he'd do but that Ross could smell when he returned. Ross told him things he didn't think anyone cared about, like how working firewood with his dad is the only career he can imagine, and, for some reason, Miners Day. Collin wanted to know details about each event and Ross, to his amazement, was speaking them.

He passes the dress-up booth for old time-y photos, a food tent with cornbread and goulash, and Boy Scout Troop 782 selling chocolate bars. Ross's wish every birthday and Christmas until middle school was to be in Boy Scouts, but his dad couldn't afford the fees and wouldn't ask for the financial assistance form. Gus told his kids that what was better than Boy Scouts was running a firewood business. Every day after school it was, This is how you start a chainsaw stubborn to start, This is how you angle the blade so the tree falls the right way, This is how you know how big a cord of wood is. Ross caught the fever in high school, but Tyler never did. For years, the idea of leaving firewood to work with concrete in flat-land Nebraska felt to Ross like jumping in a hole and letting his feet then ankles then knees turn to stone. But now he feels a lightness when he thinks about it. His life in Clayton has become thick with what did or did not happen. Nebraska, anywhere, might be a clearing.

He stops to watch a round of double jack. Three teams work in a line, the drillers swinging hammers at steel held by men who twist the steel after each hit. The hammers have heads the size of hearts.

*Have you ever tried it?* Collin had said about double jack. *You and me would be the fastest of all these guys,* he said, swiveling around from the bar to the pool players, where their cohort and mentors had condensed to only two tables.

"Three…two…!" an announcer calls.

After a final swing, the men step away, slapping backs, catching breath. The judge walks from boulder to boulder, planting and removing a measuring stick. The next four heats will make new holes in the same boulder. All you need is a hole deeper than anyone else's and you get a thousand bucks.

*We'd have to train,* Ross said. Collin said, *For sure.*

"Twenty inches, nineteen and a half, twenty-one!"

There is Bonnie Hadford, crouched on the ground with her camera snapping at the double jack teams shaking each other's hands. Ross knew she'd be here, but he still feels the heat from the rest of his body burn to his hands, a sensation that started the night of the Fourth when his brother and their cousins were spread around him, looking up at the sky, holding their breath until noise broke open behind them, and there was an emptiness in Ross's hands that he wished were filled with fire, blisters, burns.

A body was on the ground and other bodies crackled around it, towards it and back, bending down and standing up until Bonnie pushed through and Ross felt better, for one moment, like all the times he'd opened the front door and there was Bonnie holding a pan of something sweet from the oven. But that night Bonnie kneeled to the ground and then the body on the ground was in Bonnie's arms until they rose together like ghosts and folded into the backseat of their car that his dad was driving. Ross watched them drive away, Bonnie in the back, Elizabeth's head in her lap, a towel someone had brought from somewhere over her face; he watched the red taillights move up Tungsten Road like two burning eyes, then turn away. His cousins and brother were already yelling at the fireworks show over the reservoir that Ross could feel on the back of his neck as he stared at the dark and empty dirt road. His uncle came to him and said, *You cryin?* and he was. *She'll be fine,* his uncle said, but Ross knew it wouldn't be.

Every year the Hadfords order a cord of wood and never ask for stacking; Ross always stacks it anyway, when he knows no one is home. He's entering men's hand mucking to leave something to Elizabeth. He'll mail the five hundred dollars cash to her before they leave town, from the Merrill post office. He won't write anything else on the envelope. That way, no one will be able to trace it back to him and no one will make her think that it's not for her.

He pushes his way through the thick crowd trying to find a spot filled with only tourists, but he traps himself behind a group of local teens. Karly Krane is one of them, a little punk who used to play with Elizabeth—she was there the night of the Fourth. Karly and Elizabeth used to spy on Ross and Tyler through the trees while they chopped wood, even after what happened to Elizabeth's eye. Sometimes Karly popped out trying to scare them, but Elizabeth always stayed hidden.

"Hey, Ross," Karly says. She used to wear giant T-shirts big enough to be dresses, but now she has on something tight and tiny that shows her belly button. Her hair is up in a ponytail, dyed black, and her eyes are rimmed red; she's probably stoned.

"Afternoon," he says.

"Hey, is Tyler here?" she says.

"Not that I know of."

"Do you have a cigarette?" Karly pulls out her ponytail in a way that looks like it hurts. The kids with her, a boy and a girl, each have a can of Mountain Dew. The boy is the Navajo kid who Ross and his dad picked up once on their way back from a delivery. The boy and his mom were out in the middle of nowhere, way down Ridgeback Road. They weren't hitching, but when Ross's dad offered a ride to town, they took it. They sat in the back of the truck and Ross could see the mom's hair in the passenger-side mirror, long and black and getting pushed around by the wind.

"Don't smoke," Ross says. He looks over the crowd to see if the woman from Wyoming is still at it with hand mucking. It is someone else, a guy who looks older than Ross's dad. He has a solid shoveling rhythm, a good pace, and isn't throwing dirt out instead of in, like some people do when excited. Even so, Ross can see that his own work will be faster.

"So there's the high school grad party tonight," Karly says, working her hair back up. "Tyler's coming, right? You should come too, but it's like, we don't have anything to drink. Could you get us some stuff from High Spirits?"

The man pushes against the wagon full of dirt. His body angles low to the ground but the wagon sticks.

Ross wants to ask if Elizabeth is going. He has tried to look out for her, but she's never needed looking out for in ways he could help with. He has never seen her bullied or made fun of for the glasses she had to wear to protect her healthy eye; instead, other kids seemed to have let her slide away, as if her eye prevented not her from seeing, but others from seeing her.

"I'm not sure Jeff would appreciate that," Ross says.

"Seriously?" Karly says, and Ross doesn't need to hear the rest. He looks at the trampled grass and puts his feet where other feet are not. He hears Karly say *Wow, okay, bye*, and he drills into the even-thicker crowd toward hand mucking.

The wagon gives and the man pushes like a train down the tracks and off the edge.

"Ten minutes, five seconds!" the announcer calls.

One more until Ross.

Bonnie waves at him from the other side of the arena. She is short, just up to his dad's chest, but the crowd can't hide her. She wears a red sweater, and her braid sits on one shoulder like a rope. This morning, Bonnie knocked on the door of the main house and when he went in to shower he saw a pan of coffee cake, the kind with the crumbly cinnamon and sugar on top he remembers from when he was little.

Ross pretends not to see her by scanning the times in the men's category that are displayed on the sign-up table, focusing on what he needs to beat. As far as Ross knows, Bonnie and Vander are the only people in Clayton who know that they are moving. His dad doesn't have friends, and the only people who might notice when Ross is gone are the dozen or so regular customers that get their wood every year and will be getting a notice sent to their address the day that they leave. He called the coordinator with Merrill County Fire to be taken off the list; she said, *We're so sorry to see you go, but congratulations on your next step!* Collin might never know since he and Ross seem to be choosing different monthly trainings.

That night at the pool hall, after Collin ordered a fourth beer, he started telling Ross why he wanted to fight fires. *Fire is the only natural phenomenon that people think they can stop,* he said. *But we can't stop fire any more than we can stop a hurricane.*

Then someone called out, *Hey Lovebirds, one of you's gotta fill in,* from the pool table and Collin jumped up right away. Ross left without saying goodbye, without learning why Collin wanted to fight fires despite its impossibility. He didn't intend to leave, but when he came out of the bathroom and looked down the long hall that was filling up with people and saw that his seat at the bar was taken by someone else and that a small group formed around Collin, who described something while using his hands in the air, it was easier to step out the door to the parking lot full of trucks, not people.

Bonnie is navigating the crowd at the edge of the hand mucking arena, making her way toward Ross as the mucker working the track labors and people cheer him on. Ross moves with her in the opposite direction, keeping pace like working a double hand saw. The reservoir behind them is its deepest blue, sharpened with snowmelt.

The mucker pushes the wagon full of dirt over the rail. He is huge mostly in a wide way and wears an apron of sweat.

"R. Lucero?" The announcer holds up his hand to the crowd. Ross wipes his hands on his shirt. The kid volunteers lift the wagon back on the tracks.

"Yes, sir." Ross raises his hand.

The announcer waves Ross toward the wagon and chalks a

line on its side. "Dirt's gotta be all the way to the line and I'll be right here next to you to say *okay* when you can push."

"Yes, sir." Ross stares at the track and wagon and dirt. Thinks, *empty. Empty.*

"Ready?" A shovel is pushed into his hands. "No gloves?"

"No, sir."

The announcer speaks through the megaphone and there is Vander Troy with his arms crossed, Bonnie with a camera, and hundreds of people who live in Clayton that Ross must have walked by hundreds of times without seeing or being seen.

"Muck!"

The noise in the park surges but he swallows it, and his muscles and blood and bones move on their own. He sees only dirt in a pile, dirt in the shovel, dirt in the wagon, pile, shovel, wagon. He thinks about what Collin said about only containing fires as much as they'll let you. He jabs the dirt again and again, waiting for the breaking point that he feels coming when sawing through a log. Sweat falls into his eyes and burns.

"Hey, kid!" Something holds his arm. "You're good, push!"

The shovel is gone and all he has to do is push a wagon full of dirt down the rails and off, over the edge until it tips and spills, and he will get five hundred dollars that might make Elizabeth's life easier in some way that Ross cannot predict. He pushes with every muscle earned from every tree felled, every cord stacked into trucks then stacked again against walls and in sheds, every truck pushed out of snow and mud.

The wagon gives and there is no noise, no color, just a sizzling in his hands and a load of dirt moving heavy and fast because he tells it to.

When it is over, he feels strong, warmed up and ready for more work. But he has to look up now, see people, respond to them.

"Shit, kid, if you hadn't been digging to China, you would

have been way ahead," the announcer says, writing down his time.

When Ross sees his number, he knows before the announcer can say it: third place, a prize of fifty dollars. The same prize he earned more than ten years ago.

He walks away from the arena as the announcer steps onto a wooden box to give his megaphone more height. Ross can feel Bonnie watching him, but he doesn't know where she is. He walks quickly but not too quickly, trying to be a part of the crowd so that he can leave it.

Sometimes, Ross thinks about how small changes can make big differences. If Uncle Luke hadn't visited that July Fourth, if he had visited but hadn't been drinking, maybe, then there might have been a cap to put on the bottom of the tube. Something more than mud might have held the backfire closer to him, to Ross, maybe exploding in his hands.

If his mom were alive, they might not have been there with Bonnie and Elizabeth; or maybe his mom wouldn't have let them shoot off homemade rockets. Ross remembers his mom as always in the sun, shoveling snow in boots and an orange skirt. He can't remember her inside the house except for next to him in bed at the moment before falling asleep, her hand on his head fitting like a hat.

If he had walked toward the group around Collin at the bar and not away.

But none of these are small changes.

The announcer calls his name from far away. *Third prize!* he says, and he tells the same joke about digging to China with Ross's name in it. The joke hangs in the air over Clayton then gusts into the mountains forever.

# — Defensible Spaces —

## 2006

Jorge hasn't driven the Clayton-Merrill route in four years, and in that time the traffic in Merrill has thickened so much that he arrives in Clayton at 08:34 for the scheduled 08:16. This is his second loop of the morning and, like the first time, he tries not to look south across the reservoir as he approaches Clayton. If he looks south, he'll see a big tan house jutting out from the trees, behind which is a smaller house, and another small house; it is in that third house where, four years ago, he cooked his mother's recipes and left a Michener paperback. Four years ago, he had the confidence he'd be back to continue a story so long, so epic.

"Last stop, Clayton Park n Ride," he says into the bus's intercom.

The same sign, Welcome to Clayton, Colorado: Elevation 8,236, the same roundabout perplexing the same drivers he can never trust to yield. Jorge's stomach tightens: he's refused this route for four years, and in all that time he hasn't prepared himself for the probability of seeing her, the woman who probably still lives in that small house.

"I'm gonna run for coffee." Danny Mansion, Jorge's trainee, stands in the aisle with the bus still moving.

"Sit down, will ya, until I stop."

Danny sits down, and Jorge makes the sharp turn into the parking lot. They've reversed the order that buses pull in and out, but Jorge knows about it from updates.

Jorge has already gone down the list for someone to blame for why he is driving the Clayton route, but of course there is no one. Only a handful of drivers know the route, and one's husband is sick and the others are on vacation. He doesn't like being forced back. When something is over for Jorge, it is over.

He should have said no.

Danny leans out into the aisle, his elbows on his thighs. He is neatly shaven, but his jeans are full of holes and there are stains on his long-sleeve Merrill Transportation shirt. They'll make him wear the dark brown and tan uniform if he starts driving. Though Jorge wouldn't get on a Radio Flyer wagon steered by a kid like Danny, let alone a regional coach. Not that it's his fault. The kid's been training all week with Cassie, who said something in the break room about training an Indian kid who seemed to be homeless—maybe if Cassie cared more about training than gossiping, Danny would know by now not to stand when the bus is moving. And if Cassie doesn't know how to train someone by now, that's on Merrill Transit.

"We gotta set the example," Jorge says to Danny.

He maneuvers the bus next to the concrete island where the usual crowd forms a sleepy line. Off to the left, a few people mill about the Town Hall setting up a table, unrolling a banner. It is only September but people in Clayton have a lot to worry about with this election. Yes on 2A would extend residential building boundaries two miles into the west side of Red Bird Forest. It is county land that you can cut through on foot to get from the Mountain Mart to the small house he spent so much time in four summers ago. People in Merrill, who outnumber Clayton locals ten to one, are getting fed stories about new cabins for mountain retreats and a visitor center; Jorge can see already that 2A will pass. Usually he doesn't get involved except for going to the polls, but when he got a hanger on his apartment door last week, he left it there: 2A, NO WAY.

The bus exhales when he parks, and Danny jumps down the steps.

"I'll be one minute. You want anything?"

"Nope," Jorge says. "I'm leaving without you if you're not back when we're loaded." Jorge says that to all of his trainees, though it is something that he would never do.

The thirty or so passengers line up to exit, mostly tourists staying in nice hotels in Merrill and recreating in the mountains around Clayton: cyclists, hikers, leafers. Today it is mostly cyclists, judging by the spandex and the number of bikes under the bus. This is a hell of a time of year, with the leaves starting to change. The Clayton-Merrill was the best route he ever had, until it wasn't.

*Thank you.*

    *Thank you.*

    *Thank you.*

The passengers mumble, stepping down. Some of them get tangled in the swarm of kids waiting to get on, a crowd that is unusual on a regional route, especially at this time on a school day.

"Excuse me, the bikes?" The cyclists on the ground look up at Jorge, the sun reflecting off their spandex.

"Please do not reach into the compartment, wait for me to open them," Jorge says, stepping to the ground. He opens the first of the three storage areas beneath the bus, then the second, then the third. Danny should be here, learning, because the latches aren't always easy.

"Have a nice ride," Jorge says after extracting each bike.

Between the neon spandex of cyclists and the swarm of kids

something red teases Jorge's eye. A familiar red. All the movement aligns for a moment, clearing a path, and there she is: Bonnie Young, the reason he hasn't been to Clayton in four years. Bonnie *Hadford*.

She wears the same thick red sweater she's always had; right now she has the hood up and her back to him, standing away from the crowd by the bench. Does she still have the longest hair in Merrill County, hair so thick and white it seemed to talk to him when she slept?

He quickly pulls off his tuque. It is also red, maybe the exact same shade because Bonnie got it for him from the same shop in town as she got her sweater, a present for his only birthday they celebrated together. He wears it every day that it is cold enough. He steps back up into the bus and fits the tuque in the shelf to the left of his seat, next to his bottle of ice tea and a chicken salad sandwich, which he can't imagine having the stomach to eat.

Had Bonnie heard him speak to the bikers? Does she still know his voice? The way she said his name always left him with a cool, clean feeling, like mint.

He's grown a beard for the first time since his twenties, and he suddenly regrets it. It is trimmed with neat lines, but maybe it makes him look like a mess, like a man who's given up.

Passengers stare up at him, annoyed at the delay. Jorge steps down while holding up a finger, *one minute*, trying not to be noticed, and pushes the button that closes the door. They have to get on the road but he needs a minute, maybe two. He walks around the front of the bus pretending to check the tires.

Danny is returning, sipping from a Denver Nuggets travel mug. Jorge could ask him to load everyone while he hides on this side of the vehicle and pretends he hadn't seen that damn red sweater and the woman wearing it. He could walk off into the mountains and let Danny figure out the route on his own, the old fashioned way.

"Thanks, man, that was a low-caffeine emergency," Danny says. "We all set?" He raises his mug to the bus.

"Let's load," Jorge says, following Danny back to the passenger side of the bus then pushing the button to open the door. He climbs the bus's steps in front of the swarm of passengers and avoids eye contact.

His feet sweat in thick socks and the rowdy group of kids approaches.

Danny stays off the bus, sipping coffee, rubbing his eyes.

"Our turn!" Bonnie calls out and the group of girls funnels in front of her. "Tell the driver I'll pay for everyone!"

It is the same voice he hears in his thoughts when he lets himself remember the time he had a girlfriend in Clayton. But every time he lets himself remember Bonnie—her laugh that starts small then grows until it fills a room or the car or a mountain valley, her way of humming when she works in the kitchen—it never takes long for him to hear her say the phrase that sticks like a splinter in his palm: *Why does that matter?* She said it when he found out she'd never been divorced. It mattered, he told her, more times than he'd thought he'd need to, because that meant he'd been sleeping with a married woman.

So she is with this group of girls. Maybe she switched careers. She used to take pictures for the town's newspaper, which Jorge has resisted thumbing through in the breakroom for four years.

That's a lie. He has tried for four years not to thumb through the paper in the break room, but he looks every time. He knows she still works for the paper, or at least she did last month.

Half a dozen girls are on the bus and it looks like it will be a thousand more, all laughter and tangled hair and candy wrappers. On the ground, Danny stands with Bonnie at the end of the line. Maybe Danny knows her daughter, who went out of state for college and might be finishing by now.

It takes thirty seconds, or the seven months that they dated, or the four years since the last time Jorge saw her, for the girls to get in and for Danny and Bonnie to arrive at the door of the bus. Then there she is.

"Morning," she says.

He tries to smile, but maybe she can't see it through the beard.

Her face stills. Not annoyed, not regretful. Just still.

"Hi, stranger," she says. "What do I owe you? Me and the girls." She recovers to the face she uses for the world, with nothing in it for him alone. Has she ever wondered what happened to him? Taking the bus to Merrill was one of her pleasures, he knows. She used to do it just for a place to sit and think. On one of their earlier dates, she told him she'd been his passenger a few times before they officially met, and he said she must be thinking of Hank, the driver who could maybe look like Jorge. Jorge could never have driven a bus without noticing her, he said.

"How many you got there?" he says.

"Eleven students and one senior."

A happier man would make a joke: which one's the senior?

She pours in coins and the machine growls to life, churning through the money. Jorge would be annoyed at anyone else paying with dimes and quarters, but he is grateful for the noise so he won't have to say anything. She probably picked the coins from the pickle jar next to the bowl of car keys and coupons she keeps by her door.

"You adopt a bunch of kids?" he says. He could pretend to be a happier man, for the sake of the thing. "Transfers?"

"You're looking at the Interim Leader for Outdoor Girls Troop 1244," she says. "Yes to transfers, we're catching the 12 for the science museum."

She looks the same. He knows those hands with the freckles counting the transfer slips. The same white hair that can sit so still but heat up a space, like in his pickup after the video store, the VHS of a documentary about glacier formation sitting on her lap, a bag of free popcorn between them. When Jorge became so angry that his hands started shaking—he had been sleeping with a married woman for months, which was exactly the kind of person he swore he'd never be—she looked right at him, the way she'd ask a bus driver for a transfer, and said it: *Why does that matter?*

"Thanks, Jorge."

His name, the way she says it.

"You—how have you been?" Jorge says.

"Let's *go!*" a passenger yells.

"You can sit here, Mrs. Hadford," one of the girls calls out through the chatting and laughing that has faded into something far away while Bonnie stands so close. She doesn't correct the name. She moves back and the space she left fills with the girls' noise and the minutes they are behind schedule, like taking the TV off mute. In his mirror he watches her sit on the driver's side, across and back from Danny, then he releases the brake.

Into the intercom, he says, "Next stop, Meadow Road." He stares deeply into the path in front of him. He feels the way he did when he first started driving, paranoid that passengers analyze each decision, each timing of the blinker. Something could spill out that he doesn't want Bonnie to see.

Someone cuts in front of him in the roundabout. Jorge honks. He almost never honks. If Danny were paying attention, Jorge would tell him that he made a mistake, that the rules are to honk as little as possible. But in the rearview mirror, he sees Danny's back as he turns to Bonnie, their conversation lost in the noise of kids.

"Elizabeth," Bonnie says, the only word Jorge can make out.

Elizabeth is Bonnie's only child. Bonnie said she used to practice clarinet in the same window seat where Jorge read his paperbacks. There were pictures of her all over the walls at Bonnie's place, a girl with long hair and glasses who did not like to pose. The one that always stuck with Jorge was of Elizabeth sitting cross-legged against a rock with a backpack next to her, holding a sandwich, her face turned away.

Jorge and Bonnie dated the summer before Elizabeth's senior year of high school, and he only met her a few times. She lived with her father then, a man named Roy who had stories about him told like legends: Roy's family worked on the Red Bird mine generations back; thirty years ago, Roy and Bonnie built the house Bonnie still lives in, sleeping on the dirt of their property as they nailed up boards and fit together pipes; Roy moved into a shack across town when their daughter was still little. Jorge always imagined him as a kind of bigfoot, stomping around killing squirrels for food. They had been out of love for years, Bonnie said.

The way Bonnie talked about Elizabeth, he had expected them to be close as sisters, but right away he saw the space between them. Bonnie had so much love for her daughter that she needed a dam to keep it from overflowing. It meant that around Elizabeth, Bonnie was more mother than Bonnie. She scurried around to see if Elizabeth needed anything, offering to run into town if Elizabeth wanted something she didn't have.

"Meadow Road," Jorge announces, too late for anyone to pull the cord. He hits the warning grates in the middle of the pavement, something he's only done by accident half a dozen times in his career. He is now grateful for the beard, since it hides the way his face keeps flushing.

Danny has his feet in the middle of the aisle, his body leaning toward Bonnie, exactly the way a passenger should not ride the bus.

The girls' chatting erupts into laughter, one kid shrieking louder than the others; Jorge's chest tightens. He can feel the eyes of commuting passengers on his neck, willing him to do something. If it were any other group of kids on any other day, he'd have no problem doing his job. But he doesn't want Bonnie hearing him angry, hearing him be *rigid*, a word she'd thrown at him when he told her he never let anyone on the bus without fare.

He wills her to tell Troop 1244 to shut up.

"Hey, driver," a man calls out. "Can you do something about the racket?"

Jorge waves his hand, his neck burning.

"Next stop, Stair Trail road," he says into the intercom. "Ladies, please lower your voices for the safety of all passengers."

The girls' laughter explodes—this time someone snorts—and then they hush, hands over mouths. Did Bonnie hear that jerk call Jorge *driver*? Does she think Jorge is soft for doing what a passenger told him to do, or rigid for following the rules? Is she remembering the natural and easy weave of their relationship that summer, and how it unraveled and blew away that fall? Is she thinking, four years ago, ancient history?

They roll down the steepest part of the canyon and pass the trailhead that leads up to the waterfall. This is where Jorge met Bonnie. There'd been a rockslide that stopped traffic in both directions for hours, and when Jorge got out to stretch his legs like everyone else in the line of vehicles, there she was, taking photographs for the newspaper. She'd been on his bus and had her camera, had just had it repaired down in Merrill to be ready for Red Bird Mining Days starting that weekend. A week later, he found her name in the paper. They'd published her photo of a giant boulder in the middle of the road. The week after that, he found her shots from Red Bird Days. Bonnie *Young*, it said under the photos, not Hadford. Her unmarried name, for all the world to believe.

"Danny," Jorge says. "What stop's next?"

The kid spins around and catches Jorge's eyes in the mirror. He puts his hand through his hair.

"Next stop, St. Mary's Falls."

"And then Silver Hill, yeah?"

"Correct."

With the girls quiet, the air in the bus feels heavy, the way it does when two people have a lot to think about but nothing to say. They pass a line of construction vehicles slowly pushing up the canyon—Jorge will probably get stuck behind them on the next route up, putting him even farther behind the timetable. More bulldozers for more homes for more people on the road. If 2A passes, it will be the beginning of Clayton turning into Merrill. Builders will plow through the limits and leave a mess from the rubble.

"Jorge, some guys," Danny says.

Two men with thick coats lean against the Fire Danger Meter sign (Today's Fire Danger: Medium) with their thumbs out.

"Hitchhikers. And it's not a stop," Jorge says.

Hitchers try to talk their way on all the time. The way Jorge sees it, perfectly healthy guys—white guys, mostly—have the world on a platter and choose to live like that. There is no reason Jorge should break the rules on their account. If it were a woman with a baby, that would be different, but it never is.

"Silver Hill."

"What happens if you let someone on without paying?" Danny says. He speaks softly and slowly, as if he's given this question a lot of thought.

Jorge knows Bonnie feels the same way. Could she hear? If rigid was protecting the system that society has agreed upon, that if you ride a bus you pay, or that space that is officially designated as *green* can't be built over just because a dozen guys wanna make a lot of money, then Jorge is guilty. And if rigid is assuming that a woman who has lived alone using her maiden name for years before Jorge met her isn't married, then guilty again.

"It's up to you if you want to follow the rules, kid," Jorge says.

The last time he talked to Bonnie, his truck idling in front of her house after the video store, he wasn't able to look at her. He looked at the ridiculous decoration on the house next door.

It was supposed to be a turkey, wood painted in red, orange, yellow, and brown. He said something dramatic like, *It's not fair to drag someone else into your own transgressions.*

The girls are back at their loudest, playing a guessing game.

"Ladies," Jorge says into the intercom. "Please keep the volume down. Creek Park Trail."

In the rearview mirror, Bonnie's arm stretches across the aisle, her hand curling up. He's seen that arm do the same stretch out from under the quilt in her bedroom; he's seen it over the porch railing at the Inn when they'd finished hamburgers; and he saw it for the last time at the video store, when Jorge was first at the register and said to use Bonnie Young's account and the kid at the counter said, *You mean Hadford?* Bonnie was getting popcorn at the machine and stretched her arm while waiting for new kernels to pop.

Creek Park Trail marks the boundary between the city of Merrill and Merrill County Open Space. It will be two or three years before they want five miles of this land, too, or maybe then they'll ask for ten. Boundary lines don't get extended; they get crossed.

"Last stop, Merrill Station."

The bus door gasps open, and regulars already wait on the steps to exit, thirty-five minutes late.

Bonnie approaches the front. He wants to do something to show that he isn't just a driver, that she isn't just a passenger. He reaches down for the tuque but quickly pulls back his hand.

"Be careful," Jorge says when she stands next to him.

Danny is on the ground, pointing a passenger north, probably toward the outdoor mall. He has a patience with passengers, a kind slowness that Jorge never had, even at the beginning.

"Maybe we'll see you on the way back," she says, already on the ground, looking up at him. He does and does not want to see her again: it is the exact tearing feeling that made him request a route transfer four years ago.

The girls' yelling and laughing and singing swallow her up before he can respond. She waves but is tugged around before he can wave back.

They are so far behind schedule that they are closer to the next scheduled departure, the 9:04, a ghost of a bus that never was. He closes the door for thirty seconds, needing the cave of quiet behind him.

A long time ago, he worked overnight security for an office building in a sketchy part of Houston. Once when he was walking to work, not yet in uniform, some guys jumped him and stole his wallet. It still bothers him that someone he never met used his twenty-dollar bill, his license, his library card, that pieces of him were doing things that he had no control over. There might be pieces of him left at Bonnie's place, too, behind the big tan house south of the reservoir. The curled pages of *Alaska* lost on the shelf of manila folders and old phone books; surviving segments of rings from his coffee cup on the table by the window where he read before she woke up; microscopic shells from his eggs in her compost bin and now in the soil of her tiny, failing garden, frozen and thawed, frozen and thawed, frozen and thawed.

He reaches down to his shelf and puts on the tuque. He releases the air that locks the door.

# — Home Ignition Zone —

## 2011

Ashlynn is the first to wake on Christmas morning. She is up at five a.m. for ham.

Every Christmas since moving to Clayton when she was little, nearly twenty years ago, she's gone to Uncle Vander and Aunt Jolene's for Christmas. Aunt Jolene makes ham that is crispy and covered in herbs, which Ashlynn craves like nothing else. But she can't ask for the recipe, because she has decided, for the first time, to not go to the Troy ranch for Christmas.

Next, she'd choose her mom's recipe, which she remembers from an Easter, or maybe a birthday long ago, but her mom says that if she ever made ham, she probably just asked how at the deli. When Ashlynn asked, the person at the Mountain Mart deli wrote a recipe on one of those waxy white bags they give chicken wings in.

Last night when Ashlynn picked up her mom, Lonna was already in her fuzzy sky-blue bathrobe, a Christmas gift from Ashlynn when she was in high school. In the car Lonna talked about how Ashlynn's dad will never understand how much work goes into Christmas morning, about a commercial she saw for a new diet pill that would be perfect for Ashlynn after she gives birth, and about a place called Little America, where she wants to take Ashlynn's kids for ice cream cones. Ashlynn has learned to think over her mom's talking in the car, to find silence in her body that is carrying twins and too tired to listen to the same sentences over and over again. Ashlynn has learned that her mom, sitting in the passenger seat in a fuzzy blue bathrobe with a bleached-blonde halo over a gray inch of roots and bags and bags of stuff for just one night, is someone who needs to talk more than she needs to be heard.

Sometimes when Lonna stays over, she wakes up in the middle of the night and can't remember where she is, stumbling around looking for something familiar until Ashlynn wakes up from the noise and helps her back to bed.

Ashlynn turns on the kitchen light. An empty whiskey bottle is in the sink, her husband, Brady's, attempt to clean up after himself. Lonna and Brady have equal but opposite drinking problems: Brady gets excited and loud and Lonna gets confused and stubborn, both of them unmanageable. Last night Brady got on another rant about the hippies protesting clear-cutting while Lonna played Uno with Mellie, Ashlynn and Brady's four-year-old, neither of them following the rules of the game. Ashlynn went upstairs with more than half a frozen pizza on her plate, the climb feeling longer than it had the day before, the world getting less explorable with every hour that the twins live in her belly. She put on *A Christmas Story,* which she had to turn up loud because Brady continued ranting to Lonna and their bedroom is a loft.

She uncovers the ham on the counter, a pink plastic hunk the size of a baby. She preheats the oven to 350 and sits on the floor to dig around for the roasting pan in the lower drawer. The pots and pans are loud with their shifting and she hears a moan from what they call the guest bedroom: her mom fell asleep with the door wide open. Ashlynn can see her on the pullout sofa on top of the covers in the bathrobe. Before the bathrobe, she used to pass out in the same way, naked, and once in high school it happened when Ashlynn had friends over.

She closes the door and carefully gets on a chair to look for the pan above the fridge. She checks inside the oven because sometimes that happens. The oven has a meaty smell from the frozen pizzas she made last night. Her mom had slurred something about how one pizza should be enough for the four of them, but Ashlynn eats more than Brady does, especially now, so they made two. When Ashlynn is not pregnant, her mom makes sure Ashlynn knows that she is supposed to be worried about being large; she is supposed to say no to bread or drink only smoothies or get on a treadmill. Her mom used to tell her that being overweight was connected to infertility, but now that Ashlynn will have more children than her mother did, her mom will have to find another consequence.

She remembers: the roasting pan is in the back of her car. It has been there since Thanksgiving when she lent it to her friend Karly, who wanted to host a Friendsgiving in Danny Mansion's new apartment. Ashlynn can't remember if she went to the meal or not: did Mellie come? Brady? Ashlynn's pregnancy with Mellie had been hard on her mind, but twins seem to need twice as much of her memory.

Leaving the light on in the kitchen to find her way through the living room, she knocks a branch of their Christmas tree and an ornament thuds on the carpet. Their tree is always too big for their living room, but Vander, Ashlynn's uncle and Brady's boss, gives his employees a tree each year and no one has a say in what they get. There is also a mountain of presents under the tree that Ashlynn had nothing to do with, which must have come in the bags her mom brought last night, toys and more toys for Mellie even though Ashlynn tells her that toys are not what they need.

She steps into Sorels and Brady's work coat and puts the hood up. The cold snap started last night and it's snowing. Small flakes fall through the porch light until she turns it off to see the sky, somehow clear despite the snow. They rented this place for several years, starting right after their landlord's property came up for the Defensible Spaces Campaign and Brady was on the crew clearing debris for a one-hundred-foot radius from the house. Brady and the landlord got along, and soon they were renting to own, and now it is theirs. The skirt of cleared land in every direction makes Ashlynn feel not protected from fire but exposed to people driving by.

She walks by Brady's truck with the thinnest skin of snow fallen over it and opens the trunk to her car. The pan is wedged between bags of sand she keeps with her for when she gets stuck in the snow. She puts the pan on the roof and gets in the passenger seat because she can barely fit behind the wheel anymore. She sits with the door open.

She loves being awake when everyone else sleeps, a feeling she found when she started delivering for the *Clayton Clamour* on Thursday mornings. She is the first woman to drive a *Clamour* newspaper route, and while this is one tiny dot in a world of important things, sometimes she feels good about it. No one thought a woman could drive through the snowstorms or get her car out from being stuck on a far-off dirt road that snowplows sometimes miss. She knows what she's doing and after three years of having the route, other people know she does, too. She loves hurling out rolls of news, loves cards left in boxes over the holidays. She loves how it makes her part of something that isn't Troy's Trees. She loves letting Mellie sleep in the car seat in the back while she slowly reads the entire paper front page to back, spreading it to its largest on her passenger seat.

It takes her a long time to read the paper; she's not school smart like Elizabeth Hadford or Laurie Edmunds or any of the other kids who left Clayton for out of state colleges. She finished high school but barely, getting held back and failing almost everything just like Danny Mansion. She and Danny have a lot in common: despite their bad grades, they both wrote down every word the teachers said and every thought that came to them when getting through a book or a newspaper or a magazine. On the bookshelf in Ashlynn and Brady's bedroom are dozens of spiral notebooks, hers and Danny's since he didn't have a steady place for so long. She should bring them to his apartment in Clayton. She should bring them before her car has three car seats in it and it takes an hour to load everything up anytime she wants to go into town. She has tested out three car seats and the stacks of rolled up newspapers, and it will work if both twins are good in the car like Mellie is.

Maybe she should pick up her dad earlier than they'd planned, to beat the snow. Her parents live ten minutes away on dirt roads without signs: right, left, right, right. Sometimes on a down slump, Brady rants about all the driving they do for her parents, so Ashlynn doesn't bother asking him to help anymore. Though he has no problem driving twice as far into Clayton, then across town to the Troy ranch if Vander calls and needs a pair of gloves left in Brady's truck.

Even with being up so early, with having to drive over to pick up her dad in a few hours, with Brady's parents coming, with the needs of three children, two of them unseen, Ashlynn feels the same lightness she felt after calling Aunt Jolene to say they'd try Christmas on their own this year. Ashlynn wants to see if she can pull it off, sure, but really she is doing this because the thought of every child and aunt wanting to touch her belly, Brady sitting with Vander and whoever else mothing around him, her mom sneaking drinks in the bathroom, and her dad wanting to go home after thirty minutes, sounds harder than cooking, cleaning, and serving Brady's parents.

Brady says Vander's not happy, which makes Brady unhappy. Brady has worked his way closer and closer into Vander's circle, both on clearing jobs and at family gatherings. Ever since getting lead for the 2A cut in Red Bird Forest five years ago, and ever since half of Vander's younger brothers and nephews left him for the oil fields up north, Brady is one of only half a dozen family members who knows what he is doing. Vander can't worry anymore about who came to the Troys through blood or through marriage.

What Ashlynn would really like to do is be alone, all alone but with Mellie sleeping next to her while she reads a thick series of paperbacks written for teens that she's given up on being embarrassed about devouring.

Back inside, she puts the ham on the pan and then into the preheated oven, where it will bake for the next five hours. She turns off all the lights and climbs back upstairs.

Getting back in bed by Brady, it feels like the whole frame tilts with her weight. Brady doesn't notice. Ashlynn almost wants to wake him. It would be something special to make love on Christmas morning, even their slow and strange kind of love making when her body is this big. But he is in the dark stage where she can pinch and push and shove and he is nothing but a body. More and more he is just a body and it feels rude or wrong but she touches him sometimes when he's like that, not where she touches him to make love, but where she can't touch him when he's awake: his inner thigh, the inside of his arm just before the armpit hair, the space above his throat and below the line of his beard, the places kept turned in when he has the choice.

She falls asleep in seconds.

Lonna wakes up before anyone else on Christmas morning. She is in her daughter's guestroom to help with Christmas.

She pats the wall for the light switch. In her daughter's kitchen she turns on a light and can feel that the oven is on: someone must have forgotten last night. She switches it off. That's a good way to burn a place down. Ashlynn and Brady might need her around more when the twins are born.

Lonna's husband, Jay, thinks it is unnecessary to stay the

night and will come over later, but that's because men never know how much goes into Christmas morning, especially with Brady's parents coming. Lonna said she could help with Christmas Eve dinner, too, but Ashy can be stubborn and try to do it all on her own. Brady's never been a big help, drinking even more than Lonna does—Lonna returns to the guestroom to check her purse, where her water bottle of vodka is still secure.

For the first time since moving to Clayton when Ashlynn was in elementary school, they are not going to Lonna's brother's house for Christmas. Vander always puts up a show-off gigantic tree that needs a ladder to decorate, and he always has ideas for what the dozen kids, cousins, and grandkids or grandcousins or Lonna never knows what to call them, can do for fun. Christmas is always on Vander's schedule, and everyone else has to spend the day thanking him for the gifts, thanking Jolene for the food that she spreads across their gigantic table in their gigantic dining room surrounded by windows. But those two, Vander and Jolene, don't have a drop to drink even on celebrations like Christmas, which means Lonna always has to provide for herself.

Christmas should be all about making a kid feel special, which isn't possible at Vander's ranch. Ashlynn never got a Christmas to herself after they moved to Clayton, and Mellie hasn't yet, either. This Christmas will be the most special Christmas of Mellie's life, and the most relaxing of Ashy's because of Lonna's help. Mellie is an early riser and today Lonna will be ready for her so that Ashy can sleep in. Soon she won't be sleeping at all with three kids and no help from Brady. Lonna will start the coffee and the fire. Everything will be ready when Ashy wakes up.

She accidentally knocks the coffee pot against the wall. She opens cupboards looking for grounds but when she finds them she sees the filter is already full and there's water in the maker. She pushes *on*, hears it crackle. She grabs a small cup, pours in half an inch from her water bottle, fills the rest with water from the faucet.

After this Christmas Lonna will get back on track. She'll get back to AA, will maybe call Cheryl Krane who moved to Idaho so many years ago that Lonna has lost count. Cheryl is still Lonna's sponsor and still the only one who knows how low Lonna got during Ashy's last year in high school, but Cheryl has never told. Or maybe Cheryl told her granddaughter, Karly, and maybe Karly told Ashlynn, and maybe it is Ashlynn who isn't telling.

In the living room she turns on the lights to the tree. It is cold, as always, they never keep their heat on high enough. She opens the flue to the fireplace. The fire is already built, old newspaper and ripped up cereal boxes stuffed under the grate, small wood pieces on top, all ready for a match. Plenty of wood to the side, wood from Troy's Trees that Vander donates to everyone in the family, even to Lonna and Jay though they've been fighting. She has to grant Vander that much.

Matches? There they are, on the mantle. Mellie has no stocking. Lonna should have brought stockings. Mellie might expect one because that's how they do it at Vander's. The mantle looks bare. Lonna lights the fire.

She put out gifts last night after everyone was in bed and, when she plugs in the lights to the tree, they look perfect. Even Ashy doesn't know about them. Lonna made a trip to Target on that horrible seniors' van that gives her a headache, but it was worth it. She also got tinsel, which she snuck in last night. Ashlynn says she hates tinsel because it's a pain to clean up, but Mellie has never seen it, and Lonna will clean it up. Vander has cats so it has never been allowed. Lonna pulls handfuls of shiny strands from the cardboard sleeve and drapes them over the tree. Mellie will be awed. She will be awed the way Ashlynn was awed when they used tinsel for their Christmas in Texas. Ashy just doesn't remember.

If only Lonna could drive to the store and get cinnamon

rolls. She should have remembered at Target to get one of those tubes that pops open. She could show Mellie how to do it. When Ashy was little she would sit in Lonna's lap as they curled the paper off the tube, waiting for the pop, which always made her laugh her head off.

The tinsel covers the tree. It shines like a waterfall.

Lonna pours another half inch from the water bottle. More water from the faucet on top. The coffee is done and it smells perfect.

Mellie's door is still closed. None of this has woken her up yet. Lonna opens the door to check on her. She stirs. It looks like she stirs. "Ashy!" Lonna whispers. "Mellie," she says, correcting, louder. "It's Christmas morning!"

Mellie makes a cooing noise but doesn't open her eyes. Lonna leaves the door open so that when Mellie does wake up, she'll know it's okay to come outside.

"Mellie," she says again, just in case she is awake but thinks she's not supposed to be. "It's okay, it's Christmas morning!"

"Mama?" Mellie says, her eyes squinting at the light coming in.

The fire pops and Lonna realizes she forgot to put up the screen, something Ashlynn always gets worried about, as if one coal could burn down a house. She doesn't know where Ashlynn gets ideas like that; they had a fireplace for twenty years and it never happened to them. But she will put the screen up after she gets coffee. She pours herself a mug then lightens it from her water bottle and hears Mellie's heavy steps and there she is in her doorway, her arms around a stuffed polar bear. Last year at Vander's, all the kids got a stuffed polar bear and Jolene made a collage of a picture of each of the kids holding their bear and framed it for Vander's sixty-fifth birthday present.

"Mama?" Mellie says, looking up toward the loft bedroom.

"Shh," Lonna says, a finger over her mouth. "Mommy's tired, let's let her sleep in on Christmas. Look who came last night!"

She points to the tree, the tinsel, the new pile of gifts, the most magical Christmas morning Mellie will ever have, all to herself.

Mellie's eyes blossom.

"Merry Christmas!" Lonna says. "Come here, sweetie!" Lonna sits on the couch and opens her arms.

"Merry Cwismas," Mellie says and runs to her grandma, her face fixed on the tree.

Lonna gently pulls the polar bear out of Mellie's hand and whispers, "Should we open one?"

Mellie runs to the tree and picks up the box in bright pink paper with a bow stuck on top: Lonna tried to make ribbon do those curly-cues but gave up and sees that it doesn't matter now. Mellie tears into the sparkling paper and Lonna sits near her, her coffee mug on the floor.

"She's beautiful!" Lonna says when Barbie stares from her plastic case at Mellie. Ashlynn refuses to get Barbies for Mellie, but Lonna has told her so many times don't worry about the cost, she will get the accessories when Mellie wants them. Ashlynn always says it's not about that, always trying to hide how much she and Brady have to watch their money. Lonna knows now that she watched her money too much with Ashlynn growing up. But that was before Jay's disability checks and before they know it, Lonna will be getting social security. It doesn't have to be that way for Mellie.

"Her name's Barbie," Lonna says. "Isn't she pretty?"

"More!" Mellie says.

"Shh," Lonna reminds. She puts the sparkling paper in the fire and flames rush up to eat it. "Only one more. Which one?"

Lonna steers Mellie toward each present that she bought and wrapped, each unwrapping followed by a flare from throwing the paper in the fire. Lonna gets up for more coffee. After filling her mug she tips her water bottle but it is empty—she hadn't started with it full, so she can look around for something of

Brady's for one last top-off, something he might have already open. She looks in cupboard after cupboard, some of them slam closed accidentally, and—here, up high above the mugs, a small collection of shooters. The first one she grabs is a vodka. She pours half of it in the mug and will save the second half for the last coffee of the day.

Back in the living room, Mellie has a book in her lap and wrapping paper Lonna doesn't recognize by her side.

"Oops, honey, we weren't supposed to open those," Lonna says, but Mellie is already flipping over the brightly-colored pages, a new edition of the one with towers of hats that Lonna remembers reading to Ashlynn.

Lonna goes to the bathroom, keeping the door open to hear if Mellie needs anything. When she comes back there are two more skins of unfamiliar paper and the area beneath the tree is empty.

"What else did Santa bring?" Lonna says, since what's done is done. Mellie has another book and some other doll that isn't Barbie stuck behind a plastic box.

Lonna hears steps on the stairs from the loft. She looks up from the floor, her back against the couch, Mellie at her side now driving Barbie in one of her new rollerblades. Ashlynn takes two steps for each stair, pausing with both feet on each ledge. She stops with only a few steps left, large enough that if someone else wanted to get by her they wouldn't be able to. Lonna has told Ashlynn all her life the tricks to control her weight, but Ashy never listened, and she has grown and grown since high school. Now she is larger than Lonna ever imagined, carrying her own weight and twins who are almost at term, her due date just after the New Year. She is like her father, he with the XXL button downs, the high blood pressure, high cholesterol, the stent. Lonna worries for both of them, their bodies getting too big for their hearts.

"What?" Ashlynn says.

"Mama!" Mellie says, dropping the new toys and running to her.

"Mom, what the fuck?" Ashlynn says.

The curse word jolts Lonna: on Christmas morning, in front of a four-year-old.

"Mama, look how Santa camed!" Mellie says, running back to Lonna's side. Lonna puts her arm around Mellie's shoulders, pulling her into a hug.

"Let's let Mommy have some coffee first, okay sweetie?" Lonna says. "Then you can show her your new toys." She pushes herself up but her legs tingle and she sits back down. She punches her robed thigh with her fist. "My leg fell asleep! Just a second, hon, I'll get you some Christmas coffee."

Ashlynn is in the kitchen, bending down for something on the floor.

"What the fuck?"

"Ashy—"

"Did you turn off the oven?" She stands.

Lonna throws more wrapping paper into the fire, which flares.

"I didn't want the place to burn down," she says. "It must have been on all night."

"I was cooking the *ham*. What time is it?"

Lonna looks around, suddenly without any idea of where a clock might be. She finds one on a tacky palm tree frame of a picture of Ashlynn and Karly. Lonna pulls the blurry digits closer to her but before she can read them, Ashlynn is in front of her and yanks the frame from her hand.

"9:17?" Ashlynn says. "They're gonna be here at noon. Damnit."

"It's still early," Lonna says.

"Not to make ham," Ashlynn says. "That's why I was up at five to put it in the oven. Fuck." She crouches down and starts flipping through pans and pots, clanging things around. Mellie throws some paper in the fire and Lonna quickly pushes her hands back.

"Don't get too close," she whispers.

Ashlynn lets the oven door drop open and starts to lift the giant pink mound.

"Hon, let me help you," Lonna says, pushing herself up again. This time her legs connect her body to the floor. "Let's just go into town and get those cinnamon rolls in a tube, would you like that Mellie?"

"It's *Christmas*," Ashlynn says. She dumps four glugs of vegetable oil into the frying pan. She lifts the ham with both hands and puts it in the oil.

"Are you sure you can you make it on the st—"

"I gotta make up for lost time somehow, hey?" She turns on the stove and leaves the kitchen without looking at the tree, the fire, her beautiful daughter sitting so happily. She slams the bathroom door.

"I want cinnamon rolls!" Mellie says.

"I know, honey, wouldn't that be fun?" Lonna sits on the sofa, reaches for her water bottle but it is empty, so light. From the corner of her eye something glows, growing and glowing and before she can squint and see what it is she hears running down the stairs from the loft.

Lonna gets up and her water bottle falls to the floor. She can see over the counter, where a frying pan holds a burning globe.

"Lonna, open the door," Brady yells. Lonna tries to understand: Brady is awake, he is in the kitchen, he is angry. Brady yells again, so seriously that Lonna's body clenches and all she can do is sit back on the sofa and pick Mellie onto her lap. Mellie tries to pull away but Lonna holds her close.

"Lonna!" Brady says, carrying the flaming pan toward them like a torch and Lonna cannot say anything, she watches it and holds her granddaughter safe.

Brady pulls at the door to the deck until there is a seep of cold air and he heaves the thing over the railing. Lonna sees it fall in a blurry arc.

Brady shakes his hands that are red and runs to the kitchen sink. Mellie runs in the opposite direction, to the deck. Lonna follows her granddaughter, who can see through the boards of the fence what Lonna can see over the railing: the frying pan in the snow ham-down, its heat spreading into the snow, a growing hole of melt.

Jolene Troy was awake before anyone else on Christmas morning. She always wakes in the dark to get the cinnamon rolls in the oven before the ham, to fill the stockings, to arrange the gifts under the tree. She made the same amount of food even though they have half the guests as usual; tomorrow, she will make someone drive extra rolls over to Lonna and Jay and Ashlynn and Brady. She has already mailed a dozen cards to those who aren't here this year. Her husband, Vander, is angry at his brothers and their sons who left Troy's Trees last fall, which has meant that Jolene has been busy making up for his hostility.

Now, half an hour before Christmas dinner at noon, the ham is on the counter, ready, and half a dozen platters are warming in the oven. Everyone tells Jolene to get a microwave but she can taste the difference and other people would, too, if they paid more attention.

There are eight children here this year, the fewest Jolene can remember. They are outside with the adults, bundled up, working on a cave dug into a pile of snow that Vander plowed together with his new ATV, a Christmas present to himself.

Jolene wants this thirty minutes before dinner to stretch into hours. When dinner starts, the happiest day of the year will go by fast, the time eaten away with the meal, and when everyone leaves there will be that charred, vacant stretch of stillness.

This day is harder every year. Not because it's getting more challenging for Jolene to get everything done on time, which it is, or because when Vander gets on the ladder to put the lights up he looks more likely to slip and fall off, which he does. This day is harder every year because the family is falling apart and Christmas has become the growth mark on the doorframe showing by how much.

Jolene has dreams at night now, nightmares in which she hurries with a roller suitcase fixed to her chair, a duffel bag on top, a backpack off to the side, a bundle of something on her head, something strapped onto her in front the way women carry their babies now, loose bags on her lap. She always has somewhere to be but she can never make it, there is always a long staircase without a ramp or a lift and something or many things fall from her or her chair and when they drop she feels it in her stomach, the sinking feeling that comes when the brain cannot make sense of what happens to the body.

The phone rings. The sound of children scrambling inside to answer makes Jolene feel better.

One of the youngest kids gets there first and she can hear him say, "Merry Christmas from the Troy residence!" the way that all the kids have been taught to answer. "Hi Auntie. Okay. Grandma!" He yells into the kitchen. "Phone!"

All the children call Jolene Grandma even though she and Vander have no children. They wanted them, and they could have adopted after Jolene's accident, but instead they take care of the kids and now grandkids of Vander's five siblings and Jolene's four, all of whom are more than a decade younger than Jolene and Vander. They have fifteen nieces and nephews by blood between them, twenty-seven if you count spouses, which Vander sometimes and Jolene always does, and ten grandnieces and nephews so far—twelve when Ashy has her twins. Jolene knows of at least two other family members, both of them from Vander's youngest brother's irresponsibilities: a niece born out east whose mother cut all ties, and a nephew, a boy named Danny who lives right here in Clayton, whose mom used to have a reputation. Vander found out about the child after his brother had left town, and when he invited the mother to the ranch, the boy was already curious and running all over the place. They only came that one time, and Vander thinks Jolene didn't see them, but she did, through the window: the woman was short, thin, and calm, and her boy was pudgy with long dark hair and kept running and running back and forth across the deck. Jolene thought he saw her once, knows he did. They locked eyes and she almost went out to him, but then his mom reached out her hand to him, starting to walk away, and he ran to her with his whole heart and tripped. She picked him up and started down the steps and Jolene heard Vander open the door, so she moved back into the kitchen and picked up the ball of dough she'd been working on the table that reaches other people's waists.

Later, Vander said she wouldn't take any money. He said Indians are proud like that and Jolene wondered where he got that idea in a town where as far as she knew Danny's mom was the only Indian.

Jolene is no fool: there are probably more children out there from Vander's youngest brother, maybe some from the next generation, too. Vander gives her money every year for the Christmas envelopes, one-hundred-dollar bills for every family member under eighteen, and he always gives two extra, even after the girl on the east coast and Danny passed eighteen. Jolene has been saving them this whole time, though they are adults now. She doesn't know how she'll get it to the girl or when she'll get it to Danny in a way that Vander can pretend he doesn't know about. He is no fool, either.

Jolene picks up the phone hanging on the wall in the kitchen.

"Cory, sweetie, you can hang up now," she calls into the living room. But Cory has already gone, leaving the cordless on a footstool. Jolene can hear the children playing through the phone line, muffled by the windows and the wire, her own house sounding far away.

"Merry Christmas, this is Jolene."

It is Ashlynn. She has been crying. Jolene can always tell.

"Just a second, hon, let me get the other line," she says. Maybe it is something with the babies, she thinks, putting the wall phone back in its cradle and pushing her chair into the living room. Ashlynn has looked ready for weeks, not that Jolene has been able to see for herself: she gets the news from Vander who gets the news from Brady at work.

"Hi, hon, are you okay?" Jolene says. She stops in the middle of the full-length bow windows that look out to the wrap-around deck, the ranch, the mountains. If she moves to the north of the living room, she can see the edge of what used to be the Gage-iro's barn, painted a tacky pink decades ago and left that way by the new owners who turned the place into a trail ride business. When Jolene has the windows open in the summer, she can hear parents tell their kids not to be scared, that the horsy won't hurt them.

"Of course, hon, you are always welcome," she says. Ashlynn wants to come over after all. Jolene can't wait to tell Vander: the news will give him that clear, alive look he gets when things happen the way they're supposed to.

"Oh, they're sick? I'll send you home with echinacea—of course we remember Brady's parents, we'd love to have them."

Jolene knows Ashlynn's mom, Lonna, Vander's sister, must be drunk and that her husband, Jay, would never come without her. She mentions echinacea to be polite.

"We can open presents again for Mellie," she says. "We'll wait for dinner, drive safe."

Jolene feels better. Finally, she is hurrying, pushing into an amount of time that is too short but always ends up long enough. She has to add two more leaves to the adult table for Ashlynn, Brady, and Brady's parents, she has to get out four more place settings and one more for the kids' table for Mellie. She has a few extra toys she can wrap up for her, and some candles and those nice dishes someone brought last fall, for Brady's parents.

She sees Vander in his new ATV, reversing and lowering the plow again and again to perfect the edge of snow along the driveway. There was nothing wrong with his old ATV, which he gave to his nephew. That was the thing about Vander. Even after all these years, sometimes Jolene can't pull apart what he does for himself from what he does for someone else.

After the accident, Vander made sure everything in this place would let her see as much of the world as possible. He wanted to build her a ramp but she prohibited it; he built it anyway. He blames himself, even though he'd had only one beer and even though the police report recorded the other driver at fault, a man so drunk that when he woke up in the hospital he couldn't remember running the red light in Merrill, that he was in Merrill, where Merrill was. He is still in prison and Jolene writes to him in secret; her friend brings in the mail when Vander is at work and takes letters Jolene wants to send. The man in prison writes back notes that have become long and full of metaphors for god.

If there is a fire, Vander said when he built the ramp, and no one is home, you will not be trapped. If there is a fire and no one is home, Jolene sometimes thinks, I will still be home.

# — Fanning Effect —

## 2013

Karly Krane wakes up on her bed in panties and right away finds the bird shapes in the tiny holes in the ceiling tiles. A sweater hangs in front of the window so she doesn't know how long she's slept. The hair at the back of her neck is damp because of the space heater, which smells like burning metal. She stretches down to switch it off. Jeremiah always said a heater was a fire hazard in a trailer.

She stands and scoops up a sweater, drops it over her tangled hair, and pulls on black pants. In two steps she is in the kitchen-living room. The clock on the microwave says 8:40 which means 7:40. Only a few hours of sleep, then. For most of the night, the wind pushed the town around, clamping around windows, shoving snow into drifts. The guy she'd been talking with at the Inn—his name will come back to her, it always does—asked if anyone's windows had ever blown in, but no one had ever heard of it. When the Inn closed at two, she walked right into the storm, craving something to push against.

She should get something salty in her stomach to soak up anything she hadn't walked off. She opens cupboards, drawers, the fridge, the freezer, all spaces with new shapes since Jeremiah left two days ago. He was thorough when she told him to move out: she hasn't tripped over any of his rolled up socks or knocked over a half-empty tube of natural deodorant; there are no curled bags of blue corn chips in the cupboard, frozen burritos in the freezer, or smells of cheap weed and cut wood from his work clothes. All that he left from his six months of living with her are his notes and letters that she'd hidden, one of his orange lighters in the back of the cutlery drawer, and an empty spot across from the couch, where his bookcase held his clothes and a stack of George R. R. Martin paperbacks. Last week she sat on the couch while opening a bottle of wine, and he sat on the coffee table between his bookshelf and the couch and watched her face, her stomach, her breasts. Jeremiah guided her arms over her head with the bottle still closed.

What had that guy said last night? It was something about Mae Ji, a woman who has lived in Clayton her whole life, just like Karly, but decades longer.

She finds only a loaf of bread in the freezer. She shakes the ice off the bag and starts undoing the tie, then abandons the food and fills a cup with water. She drinks. She left her trailer for the Inn when the wind got its strongest, around ten. When she opened the door to the bar, a gust pushed her through and slammed the door behind her. The half-dozen customers stared, but not Jill working the bar. Jill is used to Karly making loud entrances.

There was only one unfamiliar face, a guy a decade or so older than Karly wearing a messenger cap. He was reading last week's *Clayton Clamour* that Jill keeps in the corner, the pages spread across the corner table. Karly sat at her seat at the bar, and when he said to no one in particular, *Borrowers?* the three people in earshot explained. *Everyone in town keeps their keys in the cup holder,* one person said; *over the last month, someone's been getting into cars and driving around for a while,* another said. *No breaking, just entering,* Jill said, *it's probably kids. The paper calls them the Borrowers, cuz so far everyone has gotten their car back*, someone else said. Karly said, *It is starting to piss people off.*

She chugs another glass of water. Shit, she'd told the break-up story again. That would be Jill's third night in a row hearing it. About how when Sal, Jeremiah's new landlord with benefits, confessed, Karly asked if they used a condom. Sal said yes, but everybody says yes, so Karly gave her the test: *Where does Jeremiah keep his condoms?* It took Sal forever to say it, but she got it right. And then the part about how Sal, standing on her porch, rubbing her hands over her chubby arms to stay warm, described what happened as *And then there was penetration.* For some reason Karly can't stop telling that story. She keeps telling it like she's setting up a joke and the penetration part is the punch line. No one's laughed yet, so she must be telling it badly.

She adds salt to a third glass of water, a trick that Ashlynn taught her, passed on from Ashlynn's mom. That guy in the messenger cap was the grandson of some old high school history teacher who retired before Karly could be his student. His grandson—Philip? Duncan? something that could be a first or last name—was here for the funeral. He left the corner table to join her at the bar. *He used to say*, he said, talking about his grandpa, *that a town without a history is in trouble.* When Karly told him they have a history just like any place, he said that when the mining museum burned, so did Clayton's history. *That was ten years ago*, Karly said, and he said, *Exactly.*

Karly has never liked guys who wear messenger caps. For hours he kept his body turned toward her but he never bought her a damn drink. She didn't hit it too hard but it still went beyond the cash on her, so Jill let her go home and come back to pay the full bill. Karly keeps a roll of bills in a large envelope full of letters and notes, including those from Jeremiah over the last year, so when she fished for a twenty, she had to wade through his letters. It was when she was elbow-deep in his bullshit that she got the idea to go to Sal's yard.

She breaks two pieces of bread away from the frozen loaf. She has butter, too. No toaster, but a frying pan. She starts her gas burner and puts a slice of butter in the pan. She's starting to put on weight and is thinking more and more about the things Ashlynn told her, the tricks Ashlynn's mom tried to teach her about staying thin that Karly never used to need. Bread and butter isn't one of them.

When she got back to the Inn with the money and a reusable Mountain Mart bag full of Jeremiah's notes, Duncan Wilson, whatever his name was, was gone, thank god. It was a relief, but the relief happened alongside knowing that if this were five years ago, he would not have left, he would have waited for her. Five years ago, he would have insisted on walking her home; five years ago, he would have bought all her drinks. She can feel the way people look at her starting to change. She is fading into the background, settling into the role of rambling small-town barfly.

At the end of the night, it was just Karly and Jill with nothing left to talk about. When Karly left she walked around for hours, every street to herself—and then the wind stopped. Drifts of snow sculpted around walls and the sides of cars and Karly discovered the new town that any heavy weather leaves. She walked and walked with the bag full of letters and notes, knowing she'd end up at Sal's where Jeremiah now sleeps. With the stillness after a wind like that, the moon lights the white drifts like lamps.

There was something else—something else about what Duncan Wilson Philip, whatever, had said from under his stupid messenger cap. Something that had to do with Sal's yard. But something also about Mae?

The bread and butter in the pan begins to smell like toast. She leaves it on low and goes to pee, splashes water on her face. There is no mirror in her bathroom, something all the guys who have stayed here notice more than she expects them to.

The gate to Sal's yard had hung open and Karly walked right through, picking up the dented trash can and carrying it with her to the middle of the yard. She twisted the bin into a snowdrift, then filled it with newspaper from the box of recycling, which Sal is stupid enough to leave outside, dirty cans of beans and salsa jars calling out to bears or neighborhood dogs. It was the same newspaper that Jill had at the bar, a picture of someone's Subaru parked at an angle near the reservoir, its doors hanging open. *Borrowers: When, How, and Why?* the headline asked. She crumpled all the pages into sloppy flowers then tossed them into a bouquet whose cracks she filled with Jeremiah's notes in one quick dump of the bag. Each of them had her initials drawn in intricate entanglements that she used to think was a show of his devotion to her, until she saw him doing the same thing with Clayton, Colorado, Mountain Mart, and Troy's Trees on the back of the envelope holding one of his paychecks.

In Sal's backyard, split wood was stacked against the wall under a rickety wooden awning. Maybe she'd ordered the wood from Troy's Trees. Maybe Jeremiah delivered the order, helped her stack it without charging her. Maybe she paid with penetration.

Karly added small pieces from the woodpile to the trash can, flicked on Jeremiah's orange lighter, and watched the flames eat.

She remembers these moments in images, which is how she always remembers things when she's drunk: it is never a movie, always a photo album. Gate, trash can, paper, wood, lighter.

She turns off the stove and puts the pieces of butter toast on a plate. She steps into boots, gets into her jacket, opens the screen, which is still ripped from drunk Jeremiah last summer, then the metal door, and there is Danny Mansion.

"Morning," he says, without turning around. He wears the baggy hoodie he always wears since she gave it to him for his birthday in October. She found it at a head shop in Merrill and wasn't sure if he'd like it.

Danny came with her to the Inn the first two nights after Jeremiah left, even though he doesn't drink. Last night she said she was going to bed early, but they both knew that was never true. Even when she's wrapped so thickly in her own problems, she can see out far enough to know when Danny needs a break from holding her up.

She sits next to him on her steps and offers him a piece of bread.

"Fancy," he says. He rips off a small piece, leaving the rest for her.

She and Danny are both good in the cold. They know how to sit still, that if you don't fight it, it won't fight you. She knows he needs time with his coffee before she should say much of anything, so she pretends to smoke a cigarette while he sips from his mug. She does this every time she quits smoking, sits on her steps for as long as it takes to finish one, sometimes two.

She knows Danny will understand anything she tells him, but she doesn't know how to tell about starting the fire last night. It started quickly in the trash can, and, at first, she liked how strong and fast the heat came up; but then she imagined sitting on someone's roof and looking down at herself. She saw a woman alone in the early morning in the depths of January with nothing better to do than commit petty arson over some guy that wasn't better than any other guy. From that view, she looked like the loneliest person in the world.

She puts her head on Danny's shoulder, which is always at the perfect height.

They look across the lot at what used to be her grandma's trailer, where Karly lived until she was nineteen. Her mahmo left her the trailer as a high school graduation present then moved to Boise to expand her jewelry business with a childhood friend. She comes back to visit every year, but Karly feels like a kid for how much she misses her.

Karly almost moved out of Clayton, too. Two years ago, she decided on Merrill, not too far but far enough to have to change everything; but that was the year Ashlynn's husband burnt his hands and couldn't work so was home all day, and Ashlynn had her twins and needed a place to get away and Karly's was the place. Really, Karly chickened out. Instead, she traded trailers with Sandy, which means that Karly now lives in trailer #4, which used to be owned by a woman named Camilla. Karly remembers Camilla better than any of the other people in the trailer park who helped raise her when she was little. Camilla left when Karly was in elementary school but sent postcards for a decade, always from cities Karly had never heard of: Riga, Cordoba, Dakar. The postcards stopped coming years ago, but Karly has all of them in a collage in a frame on her wall, the wall that used to be Camilla's. It is a circularity that calms her.

A neighbor's dog climbs up a pile of snow built by the wind, and digs.

"Coffee?" Danny says.

She leaves the plate on the highest step, and they stand at the same time. Karly has never had a coffee maker, which means that she and Danny spend a lot of time at the place down the road.

They turn right out of the trailer park onto First Street. The town is still, sleeping off the windstorm. She can smell wood smoke, people starting their own fires.

They pass Wildlife Retirement Center where Danny works.

"Working today?" Karly says.

"8:30."

Karly wanted to visit him there yesterday but made herself stay away, worried she'd take her shit out on him, or on the first little old lady who got in her way.

The creek to the left is frozen shut, the ice so thick it looks permanent. What if she has been stuck in a whirlpool for years and now the water she's been living in has frozen over? She's kicked lots of guys out of her trailer before; Jeremiah was nothing special but it is fucking her up. Yesterday, her boss at the Mountain Mart caught her stacking expired containers of macaroni salad in the fresh case, and when he pointed it out, she threw one to the floor. He sent her home until further notice. Her problems are becoming more and more disproportionate, feeling larger on the inside but looking smaller from the outside. She could have three kids, like Ashlynn, or a life in San Francisco with a newborn and a fancy job as an architect like Elizabeth Hadford, whom Karly keeps seeing in grainy snapshots that Bonnie prints out from emails. In the photos, Elizabeth looks more and more like a responsible adult from a JCPenney's catalog, while Karly is getting sloppier, especially when she's quitting smoking, like now. She and Jeremiah quit together a month ago, even though the whole time she could tell from his skin and mouth that he was cheating.

She digs in her jacket for cigarettes. When there aren't any, she gets the urge she has started to get lately to grab Danny's hand. Strange how many times she's walked next to him, almost every single day since eighth grade, and she's never held his hand.

"Feeling okay?" Danny says.

A few houses down, leftover Christmas lights blink.

"Bread helped," Karly says, even though the hangover is not what he meant.

On the porch of Canary's, Mae sits surrounded by the lights, smoking. It used to be Mae and Allen here every morning, Allen with coffee, Mae with a cigarette. Allen is in Europe again to help his family. Mae never looks lonely when Allen is gone, but she does look like Mae without Allen.

"You found her," Mae says to Danny. "Some wind last night, huh?"

Karly sits next to her. Mae's hair is cut short as it can get without being shaved, a look Karly is starting to wish she could pull off.

"Any cars blown into the reservoir?" Karly says. It has been twenty-seven days, but when Mae holds out a cigarette, she takes it.

"We'll find out soon," Mae says. "How you holding up?"

"You know what?" Karly says, exhaling. "He's the last fucking one." She doesn't mean to talk about Jeremiah first thing, but she is done with men like Jeremiah and it feels good to say it. Done with men with lean muscles who "love too much," which at first means they know how to make her feel high on nothing but sex but then means that they love other people, too.

No one says anything. Has she said this before? Maybe she said it at the Inn the night after he left. Maybe she's turning into one of those drunk locals who spits out the same promises night after night, believing in them so hard they start crying when they make them, then crying again when they break them.

"Be right back," Danny says. He goes inside for a coffee refill and Karly knows he'll get her a small with two sugars and cream. People who don't know him get nervous at how quiet he can be; the patient ones learn that he is kinder about people than anyone they know.

It was about fire. The grandson of the high school history teacher, messenger cap guy, told Karly a story about fire. A story about Mae and fire. He was drinking some snooty brandy cocktail that Karly was surprised Jill had the supplies for, when he got misty eyed and started regretting how he should have asked his grandfather to tell more stories, he should have visited more, he should have helped out with the museum he'd started. *It was a Chinese kid who did it*, he said, out of nowhere. Karly had started working on one of the crossword puzzles Jill keeps at the bar—it was last week's, and someone had already taken the easy ones— and she put the paper down.

*Excuse me?* she said.

*Grandpa knew it but they never arrested her,* he said. *Some local Chinese girl.*

*How did they know?* Karly said.

*Who else would burn up a mining museum in a town this small?* but before Karly could say that she didn't think anyone cared enough about any museum to burn it down, Jill opened the door to the Inn with a rush of wind that blew napkins around the room like tiny ghosts.

"What?" Mae says.

"What?" Karly says.

"You're looking at me like you've been out walking all night and didn't get enough sleep to see straight."

"Just have a lot on my mind," Karly says.

When Karly was fifteen, Mae worked at Mountain Mart and caught her stealing a *Rolling Stones* magazine and a tube of mascara. Mae didn't call the cops but instead made Karly scrape the ice off of at least two customer's cars in the parking lot every day for a whole winter. It ended up not being that bad since half of the time Danny did it with her. But Mae knows when Karly is hiding something. Maybe this whole time, Mae has been hiding something, too.

"Saw you out early this morning," Mae says. Mae lives on the same street as Sal, but her house is not one of the photos left in Karly's memory of last night. She must have walked by, though, twice: on the way up, and after.

Maybe Mae saw her leaving Sal's yard. Or maybe Mae just knows what she's done, the way Danny just knows when Karly needs a coffee or Ashlynn just knows when the roads will be too bad to drive on.

Karly just knew Jeremiah wasn't gonna work out, but she hasn't learned how to do anything about what she knows.

She looks at Mae from an angle. She has a mole on her neck and her hair that has always been dark black now, if she turns a certain way, shows a line or two of white.

"Have you ever left this place?" Karly says.

"I go to Merrill all the time," Mae says.

Mae could have done what the history teacher's grandson at the bar said. Karly realizes now that it was the story of Mae starting the fire that had given Karly the idea to start hers.

The door to Canary's creaks open, then closed, and Danny hands Karly a coffee.

"Ms. Kris is on the move," Danny says. He looks across the creek to the Mountain Mart and its plaza, where the glowing pink sign for High Altitude Pizzas is still on and will forever remind Karly of Jeremiah, since the owner named a slice after them, the Too Broke for Two, separate toppings on different halves of a single slice.

Ms. Kris, one of Clayton's two cops, stands between her black patrol car and the station. She has a soft spot for Danny but holds a twenty-year grudge against Karly from the time she and Elizabeth got caught breaking into an old cabin outside of town. Elizabeth started crying, the cheap mascara Karly had put on her melting from under her glasses, but Karly knew it wouldn't matter. They were ordered to pick up trash from along a dirt road, and when they had two full bags someone at the station gave them each a can of pop.

Coach, a man who was Karly's PE teacher in middle school and basketball coach in high school, chats with Ms. Kris as she gets into her patrol car.

"Don't worry, Coach is here to help," Karly says. They always said his coffee has whiskey in it and that is why he carries it with him everywhere, even on the sidelines during games. Karly knows it's true because in the eighth grade he left a mug on the bleacher to talk to a parent and she dared Elizabeth to taste it: Elizabeth wouldn't so Karly did.

Ms. Kris keeps the door to her patrol car open while Coach talks, the car's exhaust from its warming visible from across the creek. She gets out, closes the door, and begins clearing her windshield, a sound that carries to Canary's in crisp, distinct scrapes. When Coach steps back, still talking as Ms. Kris works, he reveals Jeremiah sitting on the bench between the police station and the laundromat, the pick-up spot for Troy's Trees work crews. He wears the color combination Karly knows too well, a dark green jacket with the hood up and a canvas backpack. He looks thinner and taller from this distance. He approaches Ms. Kris and Coach, and Ms. Kris stops scraping to respond to something he says. The three of them look first in the direction of Mae's house, of Sal's house, of miles and miles of mountains; then Ms. Kris points across the creek, an invisible line from her hand cast and hooked onto the porch of Canary's Coffee.

It is possible that a curl of smoke from the trash can in Sal's yard was stretched by a late breeze to someone's fire detector after Karly left. Or maybe something sparked out, one small brand flying beyond the snowdrifts and into the woodpile, landing just right. Maybe Jeremiah was ripped from his sleep by a screaming alarm, or by the heat of the house, or someone banging on Sal's door. Maybe Jeremiah barely escaped and is reporting arson.

Karly's lungs crackle like she swallowed the fucking cigarette.

"Damnit," she says, coughing. "Why'd you give me this, you know I quit." She throws it on the ground and right away wishes she'd handed it back to Mae.

"You okay?" Mae says.

Danny steps down to the ground and rubs the burning cigarette into the dirt with his foot.

"Sorry," Karly says. "I'm—"

She interrupts herself for a deep breath, something Mahmo is teaching her from her meditation classes in Boise. She lets the smell of cold, splintering wood on the porch fill her body. More and more air.

"Wanna walk me to work?" Danny says.

"Easy," Mae says, sitting up in her chair, still watching the creek, but now looking to the left of the parking lot toward the half-size replica of the Red Bird structure that burned when Karly was a kid. The structure that the guy at the bar said Mae set on fire, along with the museum, when Karly was a kid.

A car races down the road below the Mountain Mart into Red Bird Park; it does a donut in the dirt field that fills with cars from Merrill on sunny days and stops in its own cloud of dust. Two kids in hoodies get out, leave the doors open, and run.

"Borrowers," Mae says.

"Is that what everyone over there's worried about?" Karly says. She looks west up Third Street, towards Mae's, towards Sal's. The road is still. Sal's place is probably as it always was, the only difference being new dents in one of her pillows, a new bookshelf crowding one of her corners, and a charred trash can in the middle of her yard.

"They went right by Ms. Kris," Karly says.

"We're witnesses," Danny says.

In the Mountain Mart parking lot, Coach and Jeremiah watch Ms. Kris get into her patrol car, watch her back out and drive the speed limit toward the exit. Jeremiah sits back on the bench.

"Should we tell?" Mae says.

"I won't if you won't," Karly says.

"Secret's safe," Danny says.

Somewhere in town, the owner of that car is waiting for Ms. Kris to come by and take them to their vehicle. Maybe they were washing their coffee cup or putting on their boots when they heard their own car drive away, a sound that is strange as the sight of a favorite jacket worn by someone else, or a former lover with his arm around someone else's shoulders.

This town, Karly thinks, has a way of holding secrets in the spaces carved out by the weather.

This town, she thinks, has a way of keeping you out of trouble.

# — Wildlife Urban Interface —

## 2015

For the first time since they met in middle school, Danny Mansion has a new secret to keep from Karly Krane.

From the front desk at Wildlife Retirement Center, he watches her walk away. She limps a little from twisting her ankle yesterday, but she still looks like she would offer help before asking for it.

The old secret he has kept from her is not a secret at all, only something that has never been said out loud: he would do, and has done, almost anything for her, and everyone knows what that means.

The woods around Clayton are on fire. At first it was like any fire that happens once or twice a year: small, but close enough to read about later if you didn't skip that page in the *Clamour*. This one has been burning for more than a week, starting ten miles to the northwest and coming, day by day, closer to Clayton. Last week, almost all of Merrill County's volunteer fire department came to help, and three days ago they used planes to drop repellant. Two days ago, the wind shifted and the fire herded east, taking with it half a dozen homes and the new development of vacation rentals. It also got half of Red Bird Forest, where Danny used to camp in summers before he could rent a place. He feels like he has lost a home, but he would never say that to someone whose walls went up in flames.

The south end of town is on mandatory evacuation notice, cell towers are down, and smoke is flavoring food and scenting showers. Those who haven't left are finding each other at the Inn, the grocery store, coffee shops, even coming by the retirement center where Danny works, for news.

The office is empty, and Danny feels the tug of a wish for someone to tell about his new secret. He pulls out the envelope from his back pocket. Thirty hundred-dollar bills. The whole of them is slimmer than he would have thought, but too thick to leave in a back pocket.

He picked up the new secret at the post office on his lunch break. Karly's grandma was sending her jewelry to sell around Clayton, a new idea Karly has for making money, and she wanted to see if the package had arrived. When Karly waited in line at the counter, he pulled out the loaf of junk flyers that had been growing for weeks in his PO box. He peeled away its layers, letting them drop into the recycling bin and almost threw away the envelope at the center. *Danny Mansion* was written in the middle with black pen, then across the top, written with red pen, *#1832*, his box number.

When he opened the envelope and saw bills printed with one-zero-zero, he instinctively counted them under the counter full of flyers for local services. Some were old and some were new. Thirty hundred-dollar bills is more money than he's ever had.

"Anything?" Karly said, coming around the corner.

Without thinking, he put the envelope in his back pocket before she saw.

"One guess," he said, nodding at the recycling bin. "Your stuff come?"

"Not yet," she said.

On the walk back to work, he kept almost telling her, or waiting for her to ask. But she hadn't seen.

"Have you told Mrs. Caldwell?" she said.

"She didn't come by yesterday," Danny said. "Maybe you should tell her."

One of the homes that burned with the wind shift two days ago belonged to Mrs. Caldwell, a resident at Wildlife. She moved in soon after Danny started at the front desk. She still owns—owned—her home off Dry Gulch, a large place she and her husband built in the seventies. Her husband died twenty years ago and sometimes her kids or grandkids stay at the mountain house, but Mrs. Caldwell hasn't been back.

"I'm told I'm not good at communicating," Karly said, standing in front of Wildlife after the post office. She wore a pair of jeans that she'd had for years, and she must not have had time to put on the powder she was starting to wear because Danny could tell that she meant the comment lightly. He loved when she didn't put on the powder to cover what she called her crow's-feet because those lines showed how much she smiled.

It was Karly who heard the rumor that Mrs. Caldwell's place had gone down, and yesterday morning she and Danny hitched out to see. They got dropped off on the highway then snuck behind the barriers closing her road. When they found her lot, it was jagged pieces of a structure standing in a sea of ash.

Without saying anything, Karly started picking up objects and moving them to one spot. Danny did the same. Melted VHS tapes, blackened cutlery, a stack of plates folded into embroidered tablecloths, small, deformed paintings behind glass frames, a mirror, two sets of keys. They gathered anything they found into the spot where a front door might have been, all of it fitting in the space the size of a welcome mat.

Karly twisted her ankle as they were leaving, walking backwards for one last look.

By now Karly must be sitting with Elizabeth Hadford, one of

the kids who grew up in Clayton but left and almost never comes back. She must be in town because of the fire, maybe helping out her mom and Jorge, the bus driver Bonnie's been dating. Bonnie's place is somewhere south of Red Bird, but Danny would have heard if the fire got it.

Karly had asked if he wanted to come see Elizabeth, too, and he is thankful to have the excuse of work. Elizabeth knows him as the person he was in middle school, Joel Troy's shadow. Danny was short and round, late to grow out of his baby fat, the opposite of Joel, who was the tallest boy in eighth grade and cut the sleeves off of T-shirts because he had muscles. In the eighth grade, Elizabeth, Joel, and Danny ditched class. Instead of hitching down to Merrill like they'd planned, Danny waited off to the side while Joel did to Elizabeth what he always did to girls while Danny waited off to the side.

He puts the bills back in the envelope and holds it on both hands, like his hands are a platter. This would be enough for deposit and first and last months' rent for a new place for him and Karly. Something with two bedrooms that they could keep affording with his steady job and Karly's new gig. Or they could take a trip somewhere. Arizona to visit his mom, Idaho to visit her grandma. Or Mexico. Or California, anywhere.

The day that Danny ditched school with Joel and Elizabeth was the first day back after the Columbine shooting. Adults were dazed the way they are now dazed by the fire. Teachers weren't getting mad, they were saying *please* be quiet like they might cry. The day of the shooting, he was in eighth grade Survival Science and Mrs. Anderson was teaching how Clayton was a Wildlife Urban Interface, a WUI, which meant you had to clear a space around your house big enough to protect it. Joel sounded it out like "woo-ee!" until everyone was trying it, *Woooo-ee, woo-eeee!* then someone knocked on the door and whispered to Mrs. Anderson and she put both hands over her mouth and turned on the TV. The camera shook, aiming at a building then at the reporter who kept turning to look behind her. Words rolled by slowly at the bottom of the screen: *Caller from inside the school is "scared" and "saw two of them, all in black."* Something dark fell from a window and Mrs. Anderson gasped.

Now there are all kinds of YouTube clips from that day. Once Danny found the exact scene they'd seen in class. Or maybe the clip had filled the place of his memory, or maybe that was what he'd seen on the news that night, which he'd watched alone in his mom's apartment, until both social services case managers, his and his mom's, parked outside. They had driven twenty miles up the canyon from their offices in Merrill. *We're just dropping by to see how you and your mom are doing,* they said. *Mind if we come inside?* His mom hadn't been home since Saturday.

A shadow fills the door and Danny puts the envelope back in his pocket. The shadow is just the sway of one of the pines outside the office. Sooner or later Mrs. Caldwell will come for coffee and to check her mail. They have a routine in which she offers him coffee and he says yes and then if she has mail, he listens to her talk about who it is from. Maybe he shouldn't be the one to tell her about her home. Maybe he should dig up the number for her daughter, a lawyer somewhere in Ohio, and have her tell her mother that, on his day off, he will get a ride out to the house she built with her husband and raised her children in and bring back what's left of it in a cardboard box.

Or maybe he could get Ashlynn to come by with her kids. Mrs. Caldwell loves Ashlynn's kids, especially the twins. Karly and Ashlynn look nothing alike, but if one is there without the other, Mrs. Caldwell thinks they are the same person and Danny's wife, and that Ashlynn's kids are his own. All of which he's given up correcting.

The phone rings at the same time that the door opens. In his ear is a frantic daughter asking *Should I come out there to be with*

*Mom* and *What if she has to evacuate where will they take her?*
In front of him is Mae, who has become the animal rescue lady
since the fire started.

Danny calms the woman through the phone and waves hello
to Mae.

Mae crouches in front of the bookshelf. She wears a Nirvana
T-shirt and an old flannel despite the heat. She used to be with
Allen, whose family owned the Gageiro Ranch until they moved
back to Europe and Allen left to take care of his parents. The
Gageiro ranch is now Happy Trails Trail Rides, but only tourists
call it that.

When Danny finished high school, a few years late, his mom
left Clayton for good, and he couldn't afford rent. When Danny
stood outside the giant pink barn at the Gageiro ranch while
Allen moved back and forth with armfuls of gear to lay on the
ground in front of Danny—a tent, a ground pad, a rusty Coleman
stove that worked—Danny could see a corner of the Troy place
across the meadow. Karly had always tried to get him to go to
one of the Troy bonfires, but Danny has avoided that place all his
life because of a memory that sometimes he thinks might have
been a dream. But that deck that he could see when standing by
the pink barn with Allen is exactly the way he dreamed the deck,
or remembers it. He is small enough that his mom carries him in
his arms before putting him down on the wrap-around deck that
reminds him of a boat from some movie he likes at the time, and
he can't help running around and around until he trips, gashing
his chin. He remembers his mom carrying him away, the empty
deck bobbing with her steps. His mom says it never happened,
but he considers the scar on his chin as proof that it did. His
mom says that stories can fill in memories for scars.

"I'll transfer you," Danny says to the daughter on the phone.
"Tell her hello. Don't worry." He transfers and hangs up.

"He doing okay?" Mae says.

Mae's dad moved into Wildlife a few years ago, and she has

never skipped a week visiting him. She has brothers in California, whom she never talks about, and her mother died a year before Mr. Ji moved back to Clayton. Danny can't remember Mae leaving town for a funeral. In Danny's memories, Mae has always been here, and it has always been just her, except for when it was Mae and Allen. That Mae had a father was strange to see, at first, until their similarities came through. Danny's mom used to work with Mae at the Mountain Mart and said that Mae never walked back from a cigarette break without gathering all the shopping carts in the parking lot, even though that wasn't her job. Mr. Ji rakes the leaves every fall and would shovel snow until his arms fell off except that Danny asks him to salt the walk after Danny shovels, instead.

"He's not wearing the mask for smoke like the doctors said."

"Not surprised," Mae says, picking out the same book from the give-and-take bookcase that her dad had picked out earlier, a Stephen King. She put it back, too.

"We got one for ya," Danny says. "Pigs."

"Pigs," Mae says. She stands and approaches the desk, taking the sticky note he offers. There is an official number in Merrill people can call to get large animals to safety, but no one gets through. Mae has worked on almost every ranch within a fifteen-mile radius of Clayton and knows who might temporarily shelter animals. Because cell service is down, people are calling landlines all over town to find her.

"Think you can save the bacon?" Danny says.

"I know I can prevent the bacon," she says. "Can I use your phone?"

He moves out to let Mae sit down, even though she never does. She pounds in numbers and he steps outside. The smoke seems worse than before but it's hard to tell. He scans the doors of the former motel: Ms. Snow, Mr. Z., Mr. Kirby, Mrs. Nolan, Mrs. Caldwell. He stares at Mrs. Caldwell's door and its current jangling decoration. She makes them herself, spending hours applying bells or ribbons or wooden apples, depending on what comes her way. About a month ago, Karly arranged to put them up at Canary's Coffee, and when Danny took Mrs. Caldwell and the other residents who could walk that far to see, Mrs. Caldwell seemed to notice only the muffins in the case.

But she loves to give the decorations away. She made one for Danny's mom and her partner, a gift for their commitment ceremony. Their piece includes strings of plastic beads, food package labels, and two or three ping-pong balls, which had mysteriously disappeared from the front office a few days earlier. It's hanging over their shoe mat in Arizona, where his mom is happy and grounded and in love.

If his mom had met Neveah earlier, Danny might never have known foster families or social workers or how to sit with a person who is trying not to fall apart. His mom, Iris Pound, tried her best to keep jobs (there was the Mountain Mart, the hospital laundry department in Merrill, the gas station, a million restaurants) but it usually meant hitching up and down the canyon to save money on bus fare and sometimes that meant getting distracted, depending on who picked her up. She told him his father left Clayton before he knew about Danny. She said that no one on earth could see Danny and leave for good.

When Danny started making his own scrambled eggs, his mom occasionally didn't come home for a few days, but it wasn't leaving him. He knew a few days before it would happen, because she'd start putting her feet up on the couch and staring at the ceiling. He'd start a pot of coffee for her and then, when he started drinking it with her, he'd make two. Sometimes if he talked she felt better. Facts written in his school notebook worked best, especially ones from Survival Science: how to build a life sled of skis and rope, how to make water out of your own pee if you get caught in the desert, how to make a defensible space for your home in a Wildlife Urban Interface. Sometimes she stared at her feet while he talked, sometimes she got up and went to the bathroom and stayed in there forever. Sometimes she'd be okay by morning and sometimes part of her went away, which meant the rest of her would have to go and find it.

He never felt scared when she left. She'd given him his own last name when he was born, Mansion, so that he'd know how to live in it by himself.

Mae hangs up. She's not the kind of person who says bye.

"Find a pig pen?" He props open the door. If the smoke is comin' in, it's comin' in.

"Got one," she says. "He's home?"

"Far as I know," Danny says. He can never tell if she's joking. Mr. Ji is always home. "Is there anything I should tell people that call looking for you?"

"Take a message, if that's okay," she says, standing in the open door. "Dang, the smoke's thick as hell."

"Tell him hey," Danny says. He watches her walk toward Mr. Ji's door then turn around and head to the smoking table on the path of dirt near the parking lot. It's still hard to think *Mae* instead of *Mae and Allen*. When Mr. Ji moved in, Allen helped Mae unload suitcases from California. Danny was there when Allen lit sage in the apartment; Mae rolled her eyes but didn't tell him to put it out.

There is no one else outside. Danny looks across the reservoir, which is the lowest he's ever seen it, the scratchy wall of the dam at the end exposed to the sun.

Danny has been emailing Allen. Allen says Danny could have a job out there if he wanted one, helping on their ranch in Austria. Three grand could get him out there and then some.

Maybe the money was from Allen. Danny turned thirty two weeks ago and the number of bills can't be a coincidence. Who would know his age and birthday but not his PO box number so that the post office staff had to write it on themselves? Who else wouldn't leave it under his door or give it to him in person? Who else had that kind of money and would think he deserved it?

Maybe Allen left it for Mae to drop off at the post office. Has she been coming around more since his birthday, trying to see if he has his new secret? It's hard to notice what anyone's doing lately, because of the fire.

Maybe he should use the money to leave for a while. Not because he needs to, but because Karly needs him to, her own secret that has always corresponded to his first one.

By now, Karly must be laughing about old times with Elizabeth. Those two were best friends before Danny and Karly found each other, which was soon after the day he ditched school with Joel and Elizabeth. After Columbine and the social workers finding out his mom was leaving again, he was placed with another foster family in Merrill, but they let him stay at school in Clayton. That meant he took the bus every day, which is why he met Karly. She would hang out at the bus stop, smoking, and he started carrying around cigarettes so they could hide behind the shelter while she puffed and he tried to talk enough but not too much. His foster family at the time had friends over almost every night, all of them smoking on the back porch and leaving half-finished sticks in the ashtray, sometimes nearly-full packs in the couch.

He goes back inside and starts a pot of Folgers.

About a year ago, a scientist from the University in Merrill came to speak at Wildlife: How to Prevent Memory Loss. One way to prevent memory loss, she said, was to try to remember things. So sometimes Danny practices. He thinks about the different schools he went to when he stayed with half a dozen foster families as a kid, trying to bring back details like wall colors, kinds of carpet, the chairs in the principals' offices. They're different in every building: Clayton, Merrill, and the three or four schools in Denver.

A Wildlife resident asked the memory scientist about tricks for forgetting. The scientist laughed and said, *Wouldn't that be nice?*

If there were mental exercises he could do to forget, he would work away the night after the Columbine shooting when they put him back into temporary foster care. He would work away ditching with Joel and Elizabeth a few days later when he watched Joel touch Elizabeth without her touching him back, Elizabeth's face changed into someone else's face because her glasses were off. He watched her heart punch out of her chest like a fist, until he realized it was Joel's hand under her hoodie.

Then, to pretend he liked what he saw, but really to try to stop it, Danny shouted out *Wooee!* and Joel's face turned up to him with the look Danny would see many times later, at bars and directed at his mom, at bars and directed at Karly, the face that men have for women that Danny is afraid will one day tip over and spill into him, creating that moment in chemistry when the last drop comes through the tube and changes the color and suddenly it will be Danny's hand moving around under a woman's hoodie without her having anything to do with it.

Several times, Karly has tried to kiss Danny when drunk. The first time it happened, probably ten years ago, he kissed her back but could tell right away that her body moved in a way that her brain wouldn't remember. Now when it happens, he gently pushes her away and makes sure she has something soft to put her head on while she sleeps it off. She never remembers the next day, which is another secret Danny has from Karly. But there should be another word for when you don't tell someone something about themselves.

The coffee pot steams and cracks, which means it's almost time for Mrs. Caldwell's visit. Danny never knows if she comes when she smells the coffee, or if he knows she'll be coming and starts brewing at the right time. But today everything is off. The coffee is done and she's not here, he has three thousand dollars in his pocket, and the world around them is on fire.

Through the open door, he sees Mrs. Caldwell at the smokers' table with Mae. Mrs. Caldwell doesn't smoke but she likes to visit. She wears baggy leopard print pants and large plastic beads.

Danny grabs four mugs with one hand and the coffee pot with the other and carries it all out to the table. He sits in the chair next to Karly's, which has splotches of nail polish on the arm that she makes when she tries to wait longer before starting another cigarette. Karly sits at this table more than anyone, smoking and calling over residents or their visitors to join her. Danny has sat here with her for days, weeks, maybe months if you add it all up.

He passes around the mugs and leaves one in front of Karly's seat. Mae pulls out a cigarette, lights it. Danny pushes the ashtray toward her. Mrs. Caldwell sits up straight, playing with her necklace.

If Karly were here, she would say something. She always breaks silence when Danny needs her to. Once at the Inn someone called him Big Chief Quiet and she squeezed ketchup on the guy's shirt.

Three thousand dollars could get Karly her own new start. She could get to Idaho and be close to her grandma. She could get a place bigger than a trailer, not need to borrow money for a while. She could take the time to find someone who treats her well but isn't Danny.

"I used to live in Red Bird Forest," Danny says. He usually doesn't talk about himself, but he needs to find a way in to telling Mrs. Caldwell about her home. "Where the fire started. Now it's gone."

Mae looks at him with a poker face, exhales. Mrs. Caldwell looks at Danny, sips her coffee, then looks at Mae.

"Where is your husband?" she says.

"He's not my husband," Mae says.

She sips.

"I told him to stop coming back," Mae says.

"You told him to leave," Mrs. Caldwell says.

Danny never knew why Allen hadn't been back for more than a year; Mae telling him to stop is the only reason he would believe.

Mrs. Caldwell looks at Danny. "Where's your wife?" she says. Danny tries to catch Mae's eye, but she looks down, puts out her cigarette.

"She'll be back later," Danny says.

"She left," Mrs. Caldwell says. "My husband left, too."

Danny prepares more things to talk about. He wants to tell them about what Allen taught him, how to take deep belly breaths when he feels lost, and how to let the feeling of being lost spread until it filled all of Red Bird Forest so that feeling lost was a way of locating himself on the ground.

He wants to tell them that he's starting to read the signs that he has to leave. It might be to Austria or Arizona or somewhere else. Karly has fuel and spark, and if he lets her have air, she might be able to start something.

But you can't explain something like that to people you see every day, so he will tell them about the different ways of putting out a fire. How it's not always just water, sometimes it's dropping repellant from the air, and sometimes it's guessing where the fire might be and digging a trench to divert it.

Danny sees Mr. Ji open his door and lean against the frame. He looks over their heads to the reservoir. The phone in the office rings.

"People leave," Mrs. Caldwell says. "Places don't leave."

Danny looks at Karly's chair and then out at the reservoir. When she comes back, she will sit in her chair and light a cigarette and drink the coffee he has already poured for her, even though it will be cold. And then he will tell them how just like there are different kinds of trees and all of them burn differently, there are different kinds of fires: surface, ground, and crown. Each of them, he will tell them, has their own way of preparing to ignite.

# — Evacuation —

## 2015

Every time Elizabeth Hadford returns to Clayton, she rolls down the car windows. Zero degrees or eighty, she sticks her hand out for air. This time there'll be an extra charge from the rental company for the smell of wood smoke in the upholstery. No matter how many times she showers, for the next week the smoke will be in her clothes, her hair, her skin.

Today, there are even fewer cars on the road than yesterday. This morning, the online report predicted greater danger: another day without rain, stronger winds. Approaching town, the big tan house still stands tall across the reservoir. Elizabeth grew up in a small house behind the large tan one, and her mom still lives there, just half a mile east of Red Bird Forest where the fire still burns. Her mom's place is just inside the evacuation zone. Yesterday Elizabeth used only half an hour of the four-hour re-entry window to rescue food that had defrosted since the power was cut. She took the food straight to the dump but couldn't shake the guilty feeling: what if the place actually burned. Today, she'll rescue what her mom would want to survive.

The burn line opens in front of her. Now they're saying it was negligent campers who started the fire, people from out of town.

The drive up from Merrill is too quick. She always feels good in a car in Clayton and wants more time with the feeling of knowing where to go and how things used to be. But whenever she gets out of the car, she worries someone will recognize her. Or not recognize her. So far, she is one for one. Yesterday, the guy at the dump recognized her, but Joel Troy hadn't. Joel stood with a clipboard at the evacuation check-in point on the turnoff a mile from her childhood home and didn't ask for her name, only the address; when he told her to be out by three, she could tell he could barely see her, the sun hitting his eyes so he had to squint. In the eighth grade, he had been her first kiss, not a good one. Yesterday, he called her ma'am.

She turns right on a dirt road that heads up to a lookout over Clayton and parks in the small lot that used to be the only place in town with cell service. Joel must not have the jagged flashes of memories of that kiss that she has: the cold, hard dirt behind the football team equipment shed and a remaining drift of snow; his tan skin showing through a large rip in his shirt; his body smelling like sweat and wet tree bark; his hands suddenly to the side of her breasts, faster than she thought they would be. He had asked her to take off her glasses, something she was never allowed to do, and she did: she knew that Joel thought he was telling her what to do, but really she was deciding for herself.

That way, when Joel Troy's tongue pushed into her mouth, marking every corner, and his hands stretched out her bra to get under it, she could distract herself with how she had made her own decision, a feeling that had nothing to do with him.

She is already late to meet Karly, but she knows it won't matter. Elizabeth comes back to Clayton once every few years, and she always caves and calls Karly even though half the time Karly doesn't show. Their lifetime of friendship has been on

Karly's terms: it was Karly's idea in the elementary after-school program to sneak back to the cafeteria's pantry and swipe handfuls of sugar from the thick paper bag; Karly's idea to break into an abandoned house in middle school; Karly's idea to steal little things from the gas station, to roll fake cigarettes full of cinnamon or whatever they could find, to stay up all night, to light fires in trash cans. It was always Karly leading and Elizabeth hovering around in the back, wishing she was anywhere else.

Karly RSVP'd yes to Elizabeth's wedding at a hotel in Merrill, but the plate for her and her plus-one glistened empty, $150 down the drain. No call, no text afterward. That should be a deal breaker, but it wasn't. They never miss a voicemail on each other's birthday.

From this lookout, she can see all of Clayton, houses like patchwork in the forest above the reservoir. She gets out of the car and stands in front of it. She sees the big tan house, but not her mom's place, which is camouflaged into the woods behind the big one. From this distance, Red Bird Forest is just next door. She can see the burnt scalp of the mountain where she used to hike with both of her parents and, later, each of them separately. Almost ten years ago, she and her mom spread her dad's ashes from the rock where the three of them used to picnic.

She takes a picture with her cell phone, a weak attempt to document what her mom would normally be recording with dozens of images from all over town. But for the first time in years, Bonnie isn't in Clayton.

Elizabeth got her mom and her boyfriend an Alaska cruise as a sixty-fifth birthday present. It is the first time Bonnie has gone on a vacation that doesn't involve staying on a relative's couch. They probably don't know about the fire yet, which is why Elizabeth flew in from San Francisco. Elizabeth has never been in Clayton without her mom here, and everything seems smaller and messier, as if her mom's presence prevented her from seeing her childhood home as it really is. The driveway barely had space to park, for example, a constriction she has no memory of. The remains of one of her forts, which she always imagined as deep in the woods, hung from a cluster of trees only a few yards from the house, either unnoticed by Bonnie or preserved like Elizabeth's sloppy second-grade acrylic painting of an Easter egg that Bonnie posts on the front door every March.

Yesterday, her quick run-through of the house felt like trespassing. In her childhood bedroom, tote bags of her dad's things, clothes, and books piled over the twin bed she slept on for more than half her life. Her mom said she'd donate all that, but it's been ten years. Boxes of other things, VHS tapes, old quilts, made piles on the floor where Elizabeth did sit-ups after deciding she was fat, blocking the space where she and Karly stood in front of the frameless mirror learning makeup and hair from magazines. She used to try to arrange the bed differently in the room, but it would only fit one way. Her own daughter's room is twice that size, and full of toys, with happily painted walls. Caitlin would exceed Elizabeth's childhood room in an instant.

She stood for a few moments in the tiny kitchen. The strange, cluttered design of the kitchen tiles still clashed with the faded wallpaper, and the sink was scratched and stained. One of her mom's raggedy sponges leaned against the faucet. She uses them until they break apart and strands of blue, yellow, or green clog the sink.

She started to go through the documents in the living room closet, knowing that her mom would want her to rescue photo albums, scrapbooks, certificates and receipts that are probably all online now, anyway. She pulled out some of the boxes, prying open their thick, cardboard wings and collaging their envelopes and folders of papers and photos on the living room floor. Some of them were labeled: 1981-85 taxes; 1978 job portfolio; 1995-97 Christmas cards; 2000-2002 recipes; a newer folder collecting printouts of some of the landscape designs that Elizabeth had drafted as an intern with the company where she now does part-time contract work; band concert programs; "Elizabeth's i stuff" like some prescient anticipation of the Apple products that would take over the world. She looked through this one quickly, finding only receipts from optometrists' offices, releases from dodgeball and other activities potentially menacing to her protective glasses.

When she was little, her neighbors were shooting home-made Roman candles and one backfired into her eye. She doesn't remember pain or details about what happened; what she remembers most is wearing the eyepatch afterwards, and how when Karly tried on the back-up eye patch, Elizabeth's mom saw and grabbed Karly by the arm. That's for Elizabeth, she said, and wouldn't let her go until she took it off. It is the angriest Elizabeth has ever seen her mom.

The only other envelope she opened yesterday had Merrill Weekly stamped on the front, containing a stack of black and white four-by-six photographs. Elizabeth sat on the wooden floor with her back against the lumpy sofa and moved the top photo to the bottom of the stack, an action she hasn't done in a decade with everything digital. A wooden house; the same house, the corners angled well, definitely the work of her mom, who knows how to photograph a building; another structure that looks like their neighbors' house—yes, the place next door, with half their house and half of the reservoir in the background, taken before the big house was built at the end of the drive; a view of half the frame of the window in Bonnie's bedroom, angling across and connecting with half a window of the Luceros'; the Luceros' window half open, two hands on its frame, pushing open or pulling closed?; open; a stomach, smooth and curved in the center of the wooden house, the glare of the window shielding the rest of the body; a stomach and breasts, framed by bare arms framed by the window open all the way; the profile of a naked woman, her head obscured; a woman's back, its muscles reaching up; the other side of the body, the back arched, breasts raised for the shower—and back to the first photo of the Lucero's wooden wall.

Elizabeth returned the photos to the envelope and put the envelope in the box closest to her, not remembering if it was the right container. She stacked it all back in the closet, wondering if her mom would notice a new arrangement of chaos. Those were her mother's pictures, and the subject must be the Luceros' mom, their neighbor who died before Elizabeth was born. They were beautiful photos, but did that woman know she was being photographed like that? Was her mom spying on the neighbor in the shower?

She quickly filled three garbage bags of defrosted food from the fridge and freezer, mostly repurposed yogurt containers marked by sticker-labels and Bonnie's scrawl, the labels ripped so that one strip could do as many jobs as possible. Sloppy Joe, hmbrgr, chknstew, Jorge'ssoup.

Passing Joel Troy with his clipboard on her way out, he called out That was fast! and he was right.

At the lookout above Clayton, Elizabeth breathes out—loud, so she can hear it, following the instructions from so many YouTube meditation videos. She gets back in the car and starts it. A gust of smoky wind pushes through the car windows. She rolls them up and starts driving into town.

She feels far away from her mom, farther than the distance between Alaska and Colorado. She has tried to reach the kind of closeness with her where she might believe her mom took nude photos when she was younger, but the attempt always collapses like a folding chair that they both scramble over to make sure the other isn't hurt. She notices the space between them in small moments, like when Bonnie asks questions about Caitlin that she might ask anyone with a child: Does she like vegetables? Is she a climber or a runner? Whenever Elizabeth wants to ask Bonnie real questions, like Will I always have an urge to leave work and pick her up? Will I always feel a tiny bit lonelier when she does things by herself? she chickens out and looks around online.

After visiting with Karly, Elizabeth will go back to her mom's house. She will have at least an hour left with today's re-entry window; she will go through boxes and closets logically and efficiently. If she doesn't save what her mom wants her to save, maybe they can talk about it one day.

In Canary's Coffee, Karly is with a crowd of people by the counter. She wears old jeans and a hoodie and has the same long hair and bright green eyes, the same command that tells everyone, no matter who is in the room, that they will hear her.

"Lizzie!" Karly pulls away from the group and limps up to Elizabeth for a hug, which she holds longer than most people. Elizabeth smells cigarettes, wood smoke, laundry detergent.

"Sorry I'm late," Elizabeth says.

"Honestly, I don't even know what time it is, this fire's got everything crazy. Is your mom's house okay? I love that house." She holds Elizabeth's wrist. Her face is flushed, like she's been running.

The group at the counter continues to talk, some of them watching Elizabeth and Karly. Elizabeth wishes she'd worn something else, anything but the collared shirt and mom shorts. She feels a decade older than Karly and everyone in there. She feels like a ma'am.

"It's okay. I took her defrosted food to the dump yesterday."

"Cuz your mom and Jorge are still in Alaska, right? She was telling me she was nervous to go." Karly steps over to a nearby couch and perches on its thick arm. She stares deeply into Elizabeth, still holding fast to her wrist. Elizabeth knows she'll get this focused attention for five minutes and then it will shift somewhere else.

"Nervous?" Bonnie never admitted feeling nervous to Elizabeth. About Alaska or anything else.

"We were talking about how hard it can be for people like us to do things like that," Karly says.

"Go on a cruise?"

"It's a cruise? Dang, I thought they were camping or something." The word cruise seems to have no place in the cluttered coffee shop, which didn't exist when Elizabeth lived in Clayton. It is salvaged sofas and found-object art on the walls behind and around them: strangled, cluttered collages.

"I thought it'd be relaxing—"

"But think about it. Every day it's just Clayton or Merrill, Clayton or Merrill and then suddenly, fucking Alaska. I offered her weed to take with."

"Right." Elizabeth tries to picture her mom smoking weed. Then, since Karly isn't laughing, she does picture it. Maybe Karly gives her mom and Jorge pot all the time. Maybe they all smoke pot together. Maybe her mom used to smoke pot with the lady next door and sometimes they became so relaxed they got naked and took photos.

"Did she take it?"

"I don't think Jorge would allow it," Karly says.

At first, Elizabeth hated Jorge, but it was only because he and her mom started dating the summer her dad got sick. Her dad didn't want anyone to know, and Elizabeth knows now that she should have told her mom sooner that he was barely eating. Instead, she spent that summer avoiding the house on Tungsten, horrified to see her mom cooking with someone, laughing, flirting, while her dad sat all alone in a run-down cabin that leaked, whose microwave surged, and where there wasn't TV but just a small, battery-powered TV/VCR-combo. She once used his place as a mind map for an exam on building codes since it broke so many of them.

After he got the diagnosis, stomach cancer, less than a year to live, he moved back with Bonnie. The owner tore that shack down and developed the lot into a vacation condo.

Elizabeth doesn't know why her mom and Jorge broke up back then; years later, Bonnie started saying Jorge and I on the phone, and now Elizabeth is grateful for him. He makes her mom happy, and, because of him, she spent more time with her dad before he died than she might have. Before he got sick, her dad had been attached to a memory from when she was four or five. Arranging her stuffed animals and dolls across her bed, she'd thought her dad was outside working on wood but when a car drove by she got scared and he was nowhere. He was nowhere for a long time, and Elizabeth tried to be nowhere, too, curled against the wall pretending her hardest to be one of her dolls.

"Can we go outside?" Elizabeth says to Karly.

"Were you gonna get anything? I've had, like, eight cups already." Karly heads to a side door, limping, fumbling in her pocket.

"I'll get something in a bit," Elizabeth says, following. "You limping?"

Karly falls into a deep wooden chair on the porch, crosses her legs, inhales. Says, "It's nothing."

Elizabeth takes the seat nearby, both of them facing southeast toward the reservoir and Red Bird Forest. From this angle, they can see the reservoir and the big tan house, but not the burn.

"This shit's insane," Karly says. Her face has gone pale and her eyes red.

"You okay?" Elizabeth says. She perches on her chair, a rusty stool.

"Fuck," Karly says. She cries. Elizabeth hasn't seen this since they were little girls; and then, it only happened from extreme physical pain, like the time they jumped from Bonnie's roof into a giant snowbank and Karly landed on a rock.

"This is home, you know?" Karly doesn't rub at her eyes or try to stop crying.

"It'll be okay," Elizabeth says. "They wouldn't let people back in if they really thought it'd come back."

"Now they're not letting people in," Karly says, tapping her cigarette in the repurposed saucer.

"What do you mean?"

"They closed re-entry half an hour ago."

Elizabeth takes off her glasses and cleans them on her shirt, but when she puts them back on, the air is still opaque. She looks across the creek to Red Bird Park and its ugly model of the mine headframe they rebuilt a few years ago. Above that and to the left she can see one wall of the big tan house. And behind that, invisible and buried by distance and trees and the big tan house, her mom's place, with its photos and second-grade art projects.

Leaving yesterday, she could see that if the fire were to get within a yard of the place it would inhale the surrounding nest of dead wood in seconds. In middle school, Elizabeth, her mom, and her dad spent an afternoon trying to get the property up to code, sawing off dead branches here and there for a twenty-foot radius or whatever was required. Her parents barely spoke, and they didn't get very far. There was something about the house that resisted improvement.

"Smoke's getting worse, god. How's Caity?" Karly sits up. "Every time I see Bonnie she shows one cute ass picture after another, she's gorgeous." She wipes her cheeks; her eye makeup bleeding only a little.

Elizabeth has a hum in her head that she knows she has to talk through. It's the hum she gets when something too big for her has started its course and can't be changed: when her father would not always be there anymore, only three to six fast, dazed months left; when her labor pains began and Will kept one hand on her shoulder while driving her to the hospital; when for the first time she wasn't there when Caitlin said a new word, "kite."

"Caitlin, she's really good." Elizabeth says. She called that morning from Merrill but they couldn't talk long: it is Saturday and Will and Caitlin are going on a picnic.

"She's starting kindergarten next month."

"Remember us in kindergarten?" Karly's eyes open, wide and green.

"Monsters," Elizabeth says.

She often wonders if Caitlin will be shy and quiet like her mother, and if so, will she be pulled into someone like Karly. Elizabeth needed someone to tell her what to do and Karly needed someone to tell.

"Mrs. Frye," Karly says. "And the missing tooth chart."

"I hated that stupid chart," Elizabeth says. "I never got a sticker."

Karly laughs with her mouth open. Her teeth, which had pushed into the world so early that she had the most teeth stickers of all the kindergartners, are stained.

The phone rings inside and the people in the cafe begin talking louder. The door to the porch opens.

"It shifted," someone says.

"Where?" Karly says, standing.

The sirens across town start to scream.

"It shifted," someone else says.

"Back to Red Bird."

"We have to leave town."

"They're evacuating all of Clayton."

Elizabeth remembers something the guy at the dump said when he recognized her with the trash yesterday: tell your mom hello. He must have always been there. He must have been there when her mom and dad first moved to Clayton and camped while building their little house that would last for decades, must have seen them drop off trash from the build, plastic wrapping from new windows, thick cans from wood stain. He must have seen her mom every month for the last forty years, whether she was unemployed, worked in Merrill or at the *Clayton Clamour*, or pregnant, with a little girl. How many other people in town know her mom in ways that Elizabeth never could? If she combines them, shuffles up the encounters and interactions and puts them in a manila envelope marked "Bonnie," would they mean anything if they sat in a box that burned before anyone opened it?

Karly pushes through the group that has moved in front of their view of the park. Elizabeth follows her through the strangers. The sky above Red Bird glows an orange heat that Elizabeth feels on her arms. People behind them are moving, Elizabeth doesn't know where, and she can feel Karly start to leave, too, but Elizabeth hooks her arm into Karly's and holds her there, on the porch, against the railing. Elizabeth keeps her there when a wave of wind comes from the north, blowing up dirt from the ground onto the porch and through their hair. She holds Karly's arm in her arm long enough for them to see the big tan house across the reservoir explode into flames.

# — Prescribed Burn —

## 1991

Two electronic screams pulse into Mae's ears, once, twice—a third is cut off with a slap of rattled plastic.

"Need help?" Mae calls back to her dad from the cash register at High Spirits, knowing he won't answer.

He doesn't.

The store is empty except for Mae and her parents, but it is the day before July Fourth, which means that soon there will be a straggling line of customers until closing at ten. The delivery from Merrill is late and they're out of customer favorites, including Margarita mix. Mae is only twenty, but once her dad passed her a cup of just the mix. It tastes like candy and Mae doesn't like sweets.

She hears her dad climb down the stepladder in the back room and set the smoke detector on the counter. She pictures him sliding out the small plastic doors for the batteries and the internal wires. She put the same model into their house last weekend and knows the trick, but he needs something to keep him busy.

"Just let Mae do it," her mom calls back. She sits on a crate in front of the open beer fridge, stocking Sierra Nevada, which people only buy when they run out of Coors. She leaves most of the cans in six-packs but pulls a few out of their plastic necklaces for singles. When her mom stays home, Mae stocks and cleans and arranges twice as quickly as her mom does, and works the register besides. But when her mom is in the store, she wants Mae at the cash register since she doesn't have an accent. Her dad doesn't have an accent, either, but he leaves the back room less and less, sometimes working numbers and writing letters to vendors, sometimes sitting on the floor and reading responses. Sometimes he's doing nothing at all until someone asks if he's okay, and then he pulls himself off the floor and finds something to be busy with.

Today, especially, Mae would rather be moving around since she has some thoughts to work out. Her arms ache from painting FlameAway on the Gageiro's new barn up at the ranch that morning, and each time she bends an arm her muscles remind her of Allen Gageiro, who helped paint even though he didn't have to. She had just started rolling the goop up the long wall, drops drumming on the tarp, when he came out of nowhere, like he always does.

"Are you *sure* that was the color my mom wanted?" Allen said. His puppy stumbled by his feet.

"She's the boss," Mae said. Earlier that summer she'd gone to the home supply store in Merrill with Mrs. Gageiro to help her buy buckets, brushes, and substances, but Mae had nothing to do with the French Rose pink and Winter Mood white.

"It looks like a giant Valentine," Allen said. He dipped another roller into the tray, starting at the other end of the wall. Allen was a senior in high school when Mae was a freshman. She never talked to him until this summer, but she has a vague memory of him being prom king, which now seems out of character. He lives on his parents' property in a trailer somewhere in the woods that can't be seen from the barn or the meadow. He is rich but doesn't act like it, which is how Mae would be, too.

"Valentine's Day, every day," Mae said, something that sounds stupid thinking about it now, behind the register at High Spirits. But he laughed.

"There's no way this stuff works," he said. The pup sniffed at the tray, didn't like it. She looked half wolf, half German Shepard, and a little bit like Allen, both of them partially the color of hay.

"FlameAway: Protecting Structures of Many Materials Since 1972," Mae said. That's what the giant poster boasted at the store in Merrill under a picture of half a house standing and the other half burnt away. *Should have finished the job* written underneath.

"Well, then," Allen said. They each took a step closer to the center of the barn wall, starting a new line with their rollers.

Mae never counted how many people worked on the Gage-iro ranch that summer, but if you included whoever put in a half day here and there, it might be a couple dozen. They'd cleared trees to expand the meadow to twice its size, built a fence around it for a pasture, put up a barn, and painted the barn. Now they are fire protecting the barn and will fill it with hay. A few days ago, Mr. and Mrs. Gageiro left for their daughter's wedding in Europe, Venice or Vienna, something like that. Allen didn't go with and Mae hasn't asked why. The day after the Gageiros return, they are getting horses.

"Named her yet?" Mae said. Allen's puppy chewed on the handle of a hammer someone left on the ground.

"Bad luck to give a name before she knows her home," Allen said. "But I'm open to suggestions."

"I don't want to curse her," Mae said. Jokes aside, her dad had chosen the names for her younger twin brothers before they knew for sure they were boys. Mae was five and remembers him coming home from the store with two red envelopes. Mae and her mom were playing dolls on the dining room table, which seems unlikely now, and her mom's belly was so big that they had to move the table away from the wall so that she could keep her favorite seat. Mae's dad placed the envelopes on her belly like it was a shelf, and inside each one was a name he had chosen for Mae's brothers, some strange distortion of Chinese tradition. Peter and Walter, chosen from a "top ten American boy names this year" list published in the Merrill newspaper her dad kept on the counter at High Spirits. Mae once asked her mom if there was an envelope for her name, too, and all her mom says is that she'd stopped her dad from naming her Susan. Mae can't say her mom never gave her anything.

The bell on the door to High Spirits dings and Gus Lucero walks in. Gus worked at the ranch, too, mostly clearing trees alongside the Troys at the beginning. Gus's sons follow him into the store the way they followed him up on the ranch. The older one, Ross, about twelve, did as much work as anyone else, and his younger brother, Tyler, eight or nine, pulled around a wagon to load up with tools or wood or sometimes water for the workers. There are a lot of things Mae likes about Gus but most of all she likes how all summer he never asked her to watch his kids. Other men did that when the work at the ranch first started, along with joking about her making lunch. But they got over it, just like by eighth grade the kids at school got over making fun of her short hair and *slit-eyes*.

Gus waves at Mae and she waves back. He turns left for whisky and spirits and Mae holds out the basket full of Jolly Ranchers to Ross. He takes one candy for himself then steps aside for his brother, who does the same, like always, even though Mae never says only one.

Gus talks to Mae's mom about the cord of wood he delivered last week. When her brothers are here, her mom always tells the family in San Francisco that the boys stacked the wood, even though Mae does it. She tells Gus *we got it all stacked*, even though, as usual, it was only Mae.

"You going to the party tonight?" Gus is at the counter with a bottle of Old Overholt rye, which he always gets unless another is on sale, and a six pack of beer, always bottles, never cans.

"Have to work," Mae says, taking his twenty-dollar bill. "Are you going?"

"Probably not," he says, fitting his change in a wallet. "Have a good night, kiddo."

"What party?" her mom says.

"A bonfire at the ranch," Mae says.

"It's July three" her mom says.

"That's what I said," Mae says. She gets up to prop open the door. When the sun begins to set, she'll close it because of bugs, but she has an hour to let the cooling air in. She leans against the doorframe and watches the parking lot. This parking lot is shared with Mountain Foods on one side and, on the same side as High Spirits, the video store, the police station, the *Clayton Clamour* newspaper office, and a laundromat, and it teaches Mae much about the town of Clayton.

A man with a dirty backpack approaches and she steps aside to let him in. She's seen him around, always wearing the same giant Mount Rushmore T-shirt, four stony heads plastered over his wide chest. She guesses that he camps in Red Bird Forest.

Watching the metronome of cars entering and others leaving the parking lot, Mae thinks back and forth about going to the bonfire. Back: so many Troys will be there; forth: Allen will be there. The Troys live through the woods from the Gageiros, and though Allen seems to like them, Mae has a different perspective. Her father has caught half a dozen younger Troys stealing from the store over the years, but whenever he calls the Clayton cops, they let the Troys go.

This morning, Greg Troy came by with grates for the grill pit, and Allen stopped painting FlameAway to help him unload his truck. She and Greg were in the same class from kindergarten until junior year, when Mae dropped out. They rode the same bus up to the elementary school, and once Greg pushed a burning lighter into a seat then pointed his finger at Mae and told the driver, *It was her*. She's never heard him say her name, and after that time on the bus, he has looked through her the way most guys her age look through her, as if their eyes cannot land on boy-cut hair, worn flannel, and baggy jeans. Mae cut her hair herself to two inches the night before starting sixth grade, telling all the kids she had to do it for a Chinese tradition and telling her mom it was to donate to wigs for kids with cancer in New York City. Really, she just felt like it. A new kid at school had asked, *Are you a girl or a boy?*

When Allen returned from the grill pit, he told her he hoped she could come to the bonfire. She can't remember now exactly how he said it, which words in which order, or how she responded: something that was a mumble and that got lost in how she could feel him watch her when she returned to painting. She's trying not to think of it too hard. Which is why she wishes her mom wasn't working tonight so that she could leave the register.

The guy with the backpack bumps into a shelf and bottles of rum rattle. Mae's mom pretends to wipe down the red wine section, but Mae knows she is there for its view of this guy. Yan Ji does not trust people with backpacks.

Mae walks to the back, avoiding her mom's stare screaming at her to *stay put*. Her dad stands on the stepstool, his hands over his head, adjusting the plastic disc of the smoke detector.

"I got the one at home," Mae says.

He has been wearing the same green flannel shirt for three days and with his arms raised up to the ceiling, she sees it's baggier on him than it used to be. His hair is still jet black but it is longer than it's ever been; Mae's mom used to trim it every week but ever since her mom brought up moving to San Francisco, it's been growing out. He is barely sleeping. Mae wakes up with the sun, and every morning the kettle on the stove is already warm.

"This one's quirky," he says.

Mae knows not to insist, which is what her mom would do. Her dad works the store seven days a week, even coming in on Sundays though they're not allowed to be open. He inherited the store from his dad, who got it from his dad. Mae's great-great-grandfather came to Clayton as a teenager after the Denver riots in 1880. His family had a small stationery store in Denver that was burned along with every other Chinese-owned business. In the last year or so, her dad has become worried about fire, but Mae doesn't know why now.

If you don't count her mom yelling back to her dad through the store, her parents aren't speaking during the day. Sometimes Mae hears them late at night, her mom going over again why they should move to San Francisco. Mae's great aunt needs taking care of, and Mae's mom has other family members there. The boys like it better there, Mae's mom always says, though Mae doesn't know if this is true. She never hears her dad's responses: maybe there aren't any.

"Mae," her mom calls. Mae returns to the counter, avoiding her mom's eyes. Her mom is back at the beer fridge, cleaning the door so that she can watch the man, now crouched in front of the bottom shelf of whiskies. Mr. Campos, Mae's high school history teacher, fills the door.

"Good afternoon," Mr. Campos says.

"Hi," Mae says. He walks toward the brandy shelf and Mae watches him with the same suspicion but with less subtlety than her mom has for the man with the backpack. A few years ago, Mr. Campos organized the mural of Clayton's mining history, which was painted by some famous guy on the wall of the high school auditorium. The painter worked at night so that no one could watch him, and during the day the wall was covered by a thick curtain. Mae's whole family came to the unveiling ceremony, expecting to see a rendition of the photo of her great-great-grandfather that they'd submitted. As her parents and brothers searched the cluttered collage of local historical figures for a familiar face, their heads tilted up, their eyes squinting, Mae stared at Mr. Campos, who stood at the podium, beaming in a brown sweater. Earlier that week he'd stopped Mae in the hallway to return the canvas bag of her great-great-grandfather's artifacts that Mae's mom made her submit to the new museum by the Red Bird mine. "We've decided these artifacts aren't a fit for the museum," he said. They'd donated a portrait of him standing with a shovel in front of the Red Bird in the 1890s, his mess kit with a looped rope tied on both handles so he could wear it around his neck, and his handwritten deed of sale for shares in the company. "I encourage you," he said, "to consider donating them to the Oriental museum going up in San Francisco."

Her grandfather's things are now in one of the fancy whisky crates they get every month with deliveries, next to the pistol her dad keeps on the high shelf in the coat closet. Her grandfather is not in the mural, but her brothers still think that he might be. They think that it is a game and that they just haven't spotted him yet in the crowd of dirty white faces. Mae can't tell if they are pretending.

Mr. Campos reaches for his favorite bottle of brandy.

"Hi, hon!" Cheryl Krane knocks on the doorframe. Her granddaughter runs to the end of the store, then back again. Cheryl wears a red-orange hoodie and her granddaughter wears a giant T-shirt in the same color.

"Hi, Cheryl," Mae says. Cheryl comes into High Spirits often but sometimes without buying anything. Once Mae crossed Cheryl on the trail by the reservoir and for no reason Cheryl gave her one of the crystals glinting around her neck. She must have been stoned, but still.

"Hey hon, where's that stuff you mix with tequila?" Cheryl calls from across the store. She is loud and singing and leaning against walls. It was from Cheryl that Mae learned what drunk looks like. Once, when her brothers were in the store, Cheryl sat right on the floor with them, asking what they were drawing, why they liked that color. When she left that day, either Peter or Walter asked what was wrong with that lady and Mae's mom said *she's sick*. "Delivery's late," Mae says. "It should be here soon, though, if you want to wait."

"Sweetie, don't worry about it, I'm just looking, taking my time. How are your brothers doing? Tell them hi for me."

"Can I have some candy?" Cheryl's granddaughter has so much energy that she has to sing her words, bouncing on her toes until Mae holds out the basket. The girl takes a handful and neither Cheryl nor Mae stops her.

"Jeff should be here soon," Mae says, knowing that this will distract Cheryl from the topic of her brothers, whom she does not want to talk about.

"The delivery guy? He's cute," Cheryl says. "Don't you think so?" She starts down an aisle and almost runs into Mr. Campos.

"Oh, Mr. Campos, I didn't see you in here," Cheryl says. She laughs but he doesn't join her.

"Small town," Mr. Campos says.

Mae is grateful her mom is distracted by the man with the backpack, who is now crouched in front of the bottom-shelf vodkas. If she'd been listening, she would have grabbed Cheryl's question about Mae's brothers, going on and on about what they were doing in San Francisco. She doesn't open up to anyone in town, but she seems to like Cheryl, even when she's "sick," because she's the only one who ever asks about the twins.

Mr. Campos approaches the counter with his bottle at the same time that the man with the backpack moves to the door and Mae's mom yells "Mister!"

Mr. Campos steps aside and Mae's mom runs out the door. "Mae!" her mom yells. "Hey, mister!"

"What?" Mae says to her mom, moving around the counter and stopping at the door.

"Hey mister, bring it back," her mom says. She starts after him and calls back to Mae, "Get the police." She is next to him now, small and quick next to his large and slow. She reaches as high as her arm goes and grabs a dirty-looking, faded red baseball cap off his head. He keeps walking, his red hair a messy flare.

"Mom, let it go," Mae says, but just then a cop parks in front of the police station that is only two doors down. Her mom walks quickly toward the car, waving the dirty hat.

Mr. Campos observes, the world his museum.

"Thief!" Mae hears her say to the officer, who slowly gets out of the car. She waves the hat in the direction of the departing Mount Rushmore T-shirt.

"Who, Roland?" the officers says. "He's harmless."

Mae thinks that now her mom will start yelling. She will start yelling with her arms flying through the air the way she does when her brothers got their candy stolen on Halloween or when Mae quit high school—but she does not. She walks quickly back into the store and hauls out the open box of Sierra Nevada, still half full. She drops it on the ground and the bottles clang. She goes back in the store then comes out again with two bottles of vodka, dropping them next to each other against the outside wall like lined-up customers.

"Mom," Mae says, but she can't say *stop* like she is supposed to say. The cop walks toward them.

"Dad?" Mae calls into the store.

"What's going on?" the cop says. Mae doesn't know his name but, on her smoke breaks, she sometimes watches him sitting in his patrol car in the parking lot, reading.

"She's fine," Mae says to the cop. "We're fine, just cleaning."

"Officer, did you know about people driving around in Red Bird?" Cheryl says. "Fools are scaring away all the birds."

"Is there a problem?" The officer looks at Mr. Campos for answers. Mr. Campos stands with his paper bag of brandy. There are already rum bottles next to the vodka, and white wine from the cooler, the glass frosty from the heat.

Mae brings a bottle back into the store and calls again, "Dad?"

Cheryl is still talking to the officer about Red Bird Forest, and the officer watches Mae's mom move back and forth. Jeff's truck pulls up with the delivery. He parks directly in front of the store, slightly on the sidewalk, his hazard lights flashing into the colors of the setting sun.

"Hey, Mae," Jeff says, jumping out of the driver's seat. "Sorry I'm late, what's—"

"Free," Mae's mom says to him, moving back yet again into the store. "You wanna buy this place, have it, free. Free, free, free." She comes back out with a pint of gin: "Free," she says, stacking it on a box.

"Hey, delivery man!" Cheryl sings. She leans against the counter in the store, oblivious to Mae's mom moving in and out. "You got that margarita mix stuff?" Her granddaughter starts climbing up the ramp to the truck.

"Dad!" Mae calls back again. Maybe he is sitting on the floor, leaning against the wall, staring at his feet.

"Mom," Mae says, *slow down* she wants to say.

"Ma'am," the cop says, and then the store screams from the inside, a scream coming from the back room and past the shelves shedding bottle by bottle. It screams and screams in steady, electronic bursts, and everyone in the parking lot turns and stares at High Spirits and the cop outside and the flashing hazard lights of the delivery truck and how what should be on the inside is growing against the wall on the outside, bottles and boxes and cans, the store turning inside out piece by piece. Mae watches them watch, their eyes wide, some of their hands billed over their foreheads even though there is no sun to block, some of them stepping closer like moths to a flame. Then the scream sputters, choked short, and there is a still silence and Mae's dad is in the doorframe, his body stopping his wife with a box of beer from coming out and Jeff with a pallet of Margarita mix from coming in.

Mae leaves. She floats away from the crowd in the parking lot like a ghost in the setting sun, no one noticing her there or not there. She walks across the parking lot and one hundred yards down the hill to Red Bird Park. She sits on one of the picnic tables by the museum, a building the size of High Spirits, next door to the headframe of Red Bird mine. She sits for an hour, watching day to dusk to dark.

A group of kids gathers on the other side of the headframe. They don't know Mae is there. If they looked in her direction, they would see someone in a black hoodie with the hood up and the tip of a cigarette travelling in arches from her mouth to the height of the table and back.

They throw snappers at the ground, here, there, each snap landing over tunnels dug one hundred years ago by boys not much older than they are. Then there is crackling from the other side of the headframe and excited whispers and someone says *oh shit* and they run up the hill. When they look back, their faces reflect a glow.

Even though in July they've already gotten more rain than all of last year, it grows fast. Flames reach around the headframe and move to the museum. Mae feeds the fire at the same moment that she sees it, flicking her cigarette at the wooden walls.

Walking away, she feels heat on her back that grows with the kind of speed that erases a century.

It could be just now that Allen lights the bonfire, which he told Mae he would do the second it gets too dark to see a person's face with any detail.

# Acknowledgments

I was lucky to have a squad of writers and readers who had my back over the long years of this collection's cranky adolescence. These supporters include, in hazy chronological order, Carol Turner (who is forever my first reader), Ani Kazarian, Jodi Lynn Anderson, Quincy Carroll, Jennifer Porter, Rebecca Troeger, Charlotte Milner-Barry, Chas Turner, Evan Sheldon, Greg Johnson, Delia LaJeunesse, Andrea Dreiling, and Anne Terashima. Special thanks to Ashley Garrison for sharing her expertise in firefighting and forest management—all errors in this regard are mine.

For the many forms of support that a child needs beyond reading and writing to become a writer, thank you, my parents. For the many forms of support that a writer needs beyond reading and writing to keep being a writer, thank you, Chris.

## About the Author

Alison Turner grew up in the mountains of Colorado, where she learned to endure large amounts of time in inclement weather waiting for buses. Her creative work appears in *Blue Mesa Review*, *Wordrunner eChapbooks*, *Little Patuxent Review*, *Meridian*, and *Bacopa Literary Review*, among others. She enjoys collaborating on projects that bring marginalized perspectives and experiences into conversations and historical records. She would follow winter forever if her special someone didn't prefer warm weather.

## About the Cover Photo

"Keep Warm" belongs to a photographic series featuring indoor furniture that sat outdoors, leaving pieces stained, worn, and consumed by wild grass and dried planted flowers. The artist pushed tensions between nature and design and between the furniture's simultaneous invitations of comfort and destruction. She surrounded the weathered "living room set" with smoke and fire, ignited the upholstery, or, as in "Keep Warm," embellished the seats reverently with candles.

Katie Crow has created visual art in various media, including surreal oil portraits, watercolor illustration, documentary child-birth photography, and conceptual macro photography. Her art is generally concerned with themes of displacement, misplaced or unstable reverence, equity, contradiction, humans' animal bodies in industrialized habitats, and moments of transition. She currently works full time at an art studio within a shelter for women and nonbinary and transgender people experiencing homelessness or poverty, where she coordinates programming to foster mental wellness and recovery through community art.

TORREY HOUSE PRESS

Voices for the Land

*The economy is a wholly owned subsidiary of the environment, not the other way around.*
—Senator Gaylord Nelson, founder of Earth Day

Torrey House Press publishes books at the intersection of the literary arts and environmental advocacy. THP authors explore the diversity of human experiences with the environment and engage community in conversations about landscape, literature, and the future of our ever-changing planet, inspiring action toward a more just world. We believe that lively, contemporary literature is at the cutting edge of social change. We seek to inform, expand, and reshape the dialogue on environmental justice and stewardship for the human and more-than-human world by elevating literary excellence from diverse voices.

Visit www.torreyhouse.org for reading group discussion guides, author interviews, and more.

As a 501(c)(3) nonprofit publisher, our work is made possible by generous donations from readers like you.

Torrey House Press is supported by Back of Beyond Books, the King's English Bookshop, Maria's Bookshop, the Jeffrey S. & Helen H. Cardon Foundation, the Sam & Diane Stewart Family Foundation, the Barker Foundation, the George S. & Dolores Doré Eccles Foundation, Diana Allison, Klaus Bielefeldt, Laurie Hilyer, Kitty Swenson, Shelby Tisdale, Kirtly Parker Jones, Robert Aagard & Camille Bailey Aagard, Kif Augustine Adams & Stirling Adams, Rose Chilcoat & Mark Franklin, Jerome Cooney & Laura Storjohann, Linc Cornell & Lois Cornell, Susan Cushman & Charlie Quimby, Betsy Gaines Quammen & David Quammen, the Utah Division of Arts & Museums, Utah Humanities, the National Endowment for the Humanities, the National Endowment for the Arts, the Salt Lake City Arts Council, the Utah Governor's Office of Economic Development, and Salt Lake County Zoo, Arts & Parks. Our thanks to individual donors, members, and the Torrey House Press board of directors for their valued support.

Join the Torrey House Press family and give today at www.torreyhouse.org/give.